The Burning Time

Carol Matas

ORCA BOOK PUBLISHERS

Library and Archives Canada Cataloguing in Publication

Matas, Carol, 1949-

The burning time / written by Carol Matas.
Originally published: Toronto : HarperCollins Publishers, 1994.

ISBN 978-1-55143-624-1

1. Inquisition--Juvenile fiction. I. Title.
PS8576.A7994B8 2007 jC813'.54 C2007-902409-2

First published in the United States, 2007
Library of Congress Control Number: 2007926373

Summary: After her father's sudden death, fifteen-year-old Rose Rives' mother is accused of being a witch, and Rose discovers that sixteenth-century France is a dangerous place for women.

Orca Book Publishers gratefully acknowledges the support for its publishing programs provided by the following agencies: the Government of Canada through the Book Publishing Industry Development Program and the Canada Council for the Arts, and the Province of British Columbia through the BC Arts Council and the Book Publishing Tax Credit.

Design by Teresa Bubela
Cover artwork by James Bentley
Author photo by Ruth Bonneville

ORCA BOOK PUBLISHERS
PO Box 5626, STN. B
VICTORIA, BC CANADA
V8R 6S4

ORCA BOOK PUBLISHERS
PO Box 468
CUSTER, WA USA
98240-0468

www.orcabook.com
Printed and bound in Canada.
Printed on 100% PCW recycled paper.
10 09 08 07 • 4 3 2 1

For Janeen, "Sister" in all things.

Listen, please, although you think you know all. One story has been told by the priests, the judges, the doctors. The women, accused, have been silenced. Now I take up my quill. I have no alternative, despite the pain remembering brings, for I am driven to tell you what really happened.

It began, I recall, with a small thing, a little thing, an old woman shouting...

chapter one

"I dreamed a fire consumed us all!" Mme Trembley shook her gnarled finger at us and screamed. "Don't you laugh. I heard the screams, I felt the pain. Don't laugh! I felt the heat! Beware!"

The entire village was out in the fields helping to harvest the corn belonging to the count at the chateau. We did this in addition to our own harvest. Many grumbled about the extra work but it was a tradition not easily broken.

My cousin Marguerite and I couldn't help but giggle as we worked side by side. Mme Trembley was a poor widow who lived mostly from fortune-telling, begging and a little animal healing. She was a bit crazy perhaps, though harmless, and sometimes her predictions did come true. But a fire consuming us all? It seemed ridiculous.

"Marguerite," I teased, "it must be you she's afraid of!"

"Rose," Marguerite called back, "you know I grew out of that years ago!"

Marguerite was well known to everyone in our village for her fascination with fire when she was little. She would gather twigs, set them on fire and watch until they burned down, often having to run to my mama, her aunt, with scorched fingers to be healed.

Soon everyone was calling to Marguerite and teasing her, Mme Trembley and her warnings quite forgotten. Through the particles of dust and grain thrown into the air by our rakes, I suddenly saw Papa's brown mare trot over the nearby hill into full view. "Papa!" I called, dropping my rake and running over the field toward him. "Papa."

He jumped off his horse, landing light as a feather. His large brown eyes glinted mischievously and he slipped both hands behind his back.

"Did you have a good trip?" I asked, panting a bit as I reached him.

"Yes, Rose, it was very successful."

"And did you find anything special for me?"

"What, not even a kiss before you ask for presents?"

Dutifully I stood on my tiptoes and kissed both his cheeks. He smelled fresh, like the forest he'd just ridden through.

"Philippe!"

"Suzanne!"

Mama was coming across the field.

"Oh, hurry, Papa," I urged. "What is it?"

"You must guess which hand it's in first."

"Papa, I just celebrated my fifteenth birthday. I'm too old for that game!"

"Are you? Oh, well," he sighed. "Then I shall have to give this present to one of your younger cousins."

I looked at his arms. Which one? I pointed to the right hand.

"Ah, you always pick correctly, Daughter," Papa said and handed me a little packet. I opened it to find a beautiful collar of embroidered white lace.

"It's wonderful! Thank you!"

I threw my arms around him and gave him a big hug. Mama came up behind me and he let go of me to take her hands in his.

"My wife, you become more beautiful every day."

Mama laughed. "And how was the trip?"

"Too long. I must ride over to our far fields to see how the work on them has progressed," Papa continued. "I'll be home for the midday meal." At that he squeezed Mama's hands, gave her a big kiss and leapt back onto his horse.

We waved to him as he trotted off, and then we headed back to our work. Marguerite and I and the other women, including my mama, were raking the hay and turning it as the men cut it down with their scythes. I remember I was happy and innocent that day, not thinking of anything but the hay I was raking in rhythmic motions, the jokes that flew back and forth between us all, and the glorious sensation of the hot sun on my face. I didn't mind the extra work.

Raymond caught my eye and winked. Then he began to cut with extra vigor. I knew what that was—a challenge. Raymond's father and my father were the wealthiest farmers in the area. Raymond and I had somehow fallen into a pattern of playful competition, so whether it was who could work the fields faster, dance better or talk more cleverly, he always seemed to be challenging me. I began to rake harder, making my strokes longer and catching more hay in the prongs as I turned it. The other boys followed Raymond, the girls copied me, and we were all soon calling back and forth to each other, joking about who was winning.

Suddenly Sylvie, the personal maid of the countess, came racing into the field. It was strange to see her there. Her skirts were flying, her apron was flapping, and she was short of breath. She ran right up to my mama.

"Madame Rives, please come, hurry. My mistress has gone into labor and the doctor, her own doctor she brought from town, says she will die and the baby too. Please, Madame. I know you can help!"

"But, Sylvie," Mama said, "I cannot go to her if her own doctor is already there. He will not want me and neither will your mistress or your master."

The count and countess left Paris every spring to live in their chateau and enjoy the warm months. Our family came to know Sylvie when Father bought land from the count's holdings. Sylvie was taken away from her regular duties by the count's secretary to run back and forth to the village with papers. Sylvie said he chose her to do it as a punishment after she'd been impertinent to him one day. Father had invited her to sit with our family on one early occasion and she liked that immensely. She used to laugh about how the punishment had backfired. She continued to pretend she hated the chore so she could be the messenger and visit us.

"For the sake of the countess, I dare to ask my master's permission, Madame," Sylvie said. "The doctor is angry, of course, but the master feels it is worth letting you try. I told him how capable you are."

"Mama," I cautioned her, "perhaps it would be best to leave it to the doctor. If the baby dies..."

Mama looked at me for a moment and nodded, acknowledging that what I'd said was true. If the baby died, she could be blamed. If she stayed in the field raking hay, she would certainly stay out of trouble. I felt immediately how dangerous the situation was, and so did she.

"If the countess and her baby are in danger and I can save them, I must try," she said finally. "Rose, will you come and help?"

I noticed that she asked me rather than just expecting me to go with her. I often assisted her in her healing work, for as well as being a midwife she was a healer too. She knew herbs and remedies for many sicknesses.

"Yes, of course, Mama."

"Please hurry, Madame," Sylvie urged. Mama and I gave our rakes to my cousin Marguerite, picked up our skirts, and followed Sylvie, running.

I must admit I wasn't thinking so much of the poor countess or the baby. I was thrilled at the chance of finally seeing the interior of the chateau. How often I'd gazed at that huge stone structure sitting at the top of the hillside and tried to imagine what was inside. The young count had torn down the old edifices and rebuilt the entire chateau. According to all the talk from the women in the village who worked there, it was filled with exquisite furnishings and decorations from Paris. The grounds alone were a wonder. We passed through a wrought iron gate, although we could have just crossed into the grounds from the fields, and down a long road that traversed elaborate gardens. I wanted to stop and smell the flowers and admire everything, but that's difficult to do when you're running at full speed. In front of the chateau the road wound around to the side, and Sylvie led us

to a door that turned out to be the entrance to the kitchen.
The servants looked at us curiously as we hurried through.
We followed Sylvie down a corridor, into a massive tiled foyer
and then up a grand flight of steps to another hallway. This
one had portraits hung on both walls. I wanted to stop and
stare at everything but had no time, as Sylvie was already
knocking at one of the doors.

"Who is it?" called a male voice.

"Sylvie, Monsieur," she replied. "I've come with the midwife."

"Enter."

Sylvie opened the door and motioned us to follow her
into her mistress's boudoir.

The bed, a big four-poster hung with heavy blue brocade
draperies, was at the far end of the room. At the front of
the room were chairs and couches, and despite the warm
day there was a roaring fire in the grate. As we entered, the
countess screamed—horrible screams that seemed to rip
through the air straight into our hearts. The count stood by
the window, looking out, shaking his head. A man who I
assumed was the doctor looked at Mama and me in disgust.
He was large, and bald, with a very red nose. Quite the opposite of the count, who was thin, with a full head of black hair
and a black beard. The village priest, Father Bernard, stood
in the corner, tall, lanky, his pinched expression even more
pinched than usual, his eyes squinting at Mama and me.

"Who let these women in?" the doctor demanded. "Get
them out of here."

"Monsieur, with all due respect," Sylvie insisted bravely,
"Madame Rives is the best midwife in the village—in fact, for
five villages around! She knows everything there is to know

about babies and birthings, and the count has agreed that she should have a look at the countess."

The doctor turned to the count. "Are you going to let this...this *servant* speak to me in this manner?"

The count continued to stare out the window. In a flat voice he replied, "You've told me they are both to die. My wife and my child. What could this midwife do to hurt the situation? You cannot kill someone who is already dead. You cannot kill them *more*." He paused for a moment. "I have given my permission. Let her try."

Mama approached the bed and motioned me to come with her. The countess had stopped screaming; she was moaning now, perhaps too tired to scream anymore, the pain was so severe. She was bathed in sweat.

"Please bring me some water, Sylvie, so I can wash, and some clean linens." Mama always insisted that we wash before we treated anyone, something she had learned from a great healer who had visited her village when she was young. This woman had told Mother that the dirt from our hands burrows into the wounds and the blood of the sick and often kills them. We both washed, the doctor snorting at us, calling us superstitious hags, and then we set to work.

Mama felt the countess's stomach, and then she felt inside for the baby. "It is turned wrong," she said.

"I know that!" the doctor sneered. "But it will not be turned right; I have tried."

"Perhaps I can try," Mama said quietly, trying to avoid an argument with him. I had assisted Mama before—I knew just how to hold the woman and position her so Mama could turn the baby. She worked quickly, as she always did, and of course said a prayer to the Virgin Mary before she began.

The countess screamed and screamed and then gritted her teeth as Mama told her to push, and she did, and finally the baby was born. Mama had to rub the baby all over, as it was quite blue, but soon it was pink and crying, and the countess was crying and even the count was crying. The doctor didn't shed a tear. He stomped out of the room, yelling back at us, "Only someone with the power of the devil in them could have saved that baby!"

Sylvie laughed at that and clapped her hands. Mama cleaned up the countess and made her comfortable, settling the baby in her arms before we left. Then, with many thanks from the count and two pieces of *gold*, Sylvie took us down to the kitchens for some ale. I hardly tasted the ale and the food as I drank in the opulence around me. Indeed, I was feeling a bit shaky. Countess and baby could easily have died, and that doctor would certainly have blamed us so he would not have had to take the blame himself. Things like that had happened in other villages, according to Mama. Still, it had worked out, and I felt very happy. And rich! Two gold coins. I knew they would make their way to my two brothers, who were traveling in and around Marseilles, working as merchants selling Father's crops. A coin for each of them to make their travels easier. And I did not begrudge them, even though I was the one who had assisted Mama, because I was lucky enough to stay home and they were forced to travel far from our lovely village.

On our way back to the fields, my cousin Christoph came running up to us.

"Aunt Suzanne," he called. "Something has happened, something terrible."

"What now," Mama sighed. She was tired. And all

too often her days were like this—one frantic message after another. "Madame Rives, there's been an accident." "Madame, my son has fever," and on and on. Still, she smiled at Christoph to let him know she was not angry at him.

For a moment Christoph seemed tongue-tied. Not at all like him. "It's my uncle," he said. "Your husband. A rabbit raced out of the field and spooked his horse. He's usually such a good rider—"

"What is it, Christoph?" Mama said, the color draining from her face.

"He got thrown. He's lying on the ground. He looks funny."

Once again Mama and I ran. I don't remember getting there really—just the fear, I remember the fear—and then we were there and Papa was lying on the ground, all twisted, his head at a strange angle from his body. Mama let out a terrible cry when she saw him and bent her head to his heart. She opened his eyes; they were already those of a dead man. When I saw that, I felt my heart would break in two. I sank down onto the dusty road and cried.

The day had started out sunny and happy. I had worked in the field, never suspecting what was to come. How could it have happened so fast? They carried him home, Mama weeping over his body. Suddenly, with full force, the precariousness of our life, the whims of fate, hit me with such terror I could barely move. How could one live knowing that disaster could strike at any moment? I followed the line of friends and relatives as my world rocked around me. Looking back on it now, I realize that it was on that day that fate pulled Mama and me into its turning wheel.

chapter two

Our family lived in a two-story house that we shared with Papa's brothers, Fabrisse and Jacues, and their wives and children. Since my two brothers, Arnaud and Guillaime, were traveling, Mama asked my uncle Fabrisse to write to them. But we did not even know when they would receive Uncle's letter, so we had to go ahead with the funeral. I missed them both terribly, especially Arnaud, who was just eighteen and had always taken care of me. Still, I had Marguerite, my cousin and best friend, and she stayed by my side—and I stayed by Mama's side, although that was difficult as Father Bernard always seemed to be there too. He hovered around her like a hawk, and although I couldn't exactly say he was doing anything wrong, something about his constant attentions seemed overdone. He *was* very helpful in terms of the funeral, and my aunts helped with the funeral meal.

The day of the funeral was a hard day. A hard, hard day. In a way I think I was so overwhelmed that I didn't start to really feel Papa's loss until much later. Raymond was sympathetic, as were his father and mother, M. and Mme Gaillac. They told Mama if she ever needed *anything,* she had only to ask. All she needed was Papa back, but there was no use asking for that.

The day after the funeral, Father Bernard sat with the family and read Papa's will aloud. The will stated that all Papa's land was to go to Mama, and in the event of her death it would revert to his three children, with Guillaime being in charge of the business dealings.

Uncle Fabrisse leapt up when he heard this and said, "There must be some mistake, Father. The land must revert to his brothers—that is always the way. Of course Suzanne is part of our family and will always have a home with us and never want for anything. The family holdings will be very large."

"That is not what the will says, Fabrisse," Mama said quietly. "Had Philippe wanted it done that way he would have stated it so in writing."

"But this is an outrage," Uncle Fabrisse cried. "The land was originally held by us all; it should come back to us."

"Philippe paid you for the land, Fabrisse," Mama said. "You know that. It was his to do with as he pleased."

"I am the eldest," Fabrisse replied. "I will decide what is best for this family."

"Now, now," Father Bernard said. "Fabrisse, there is no use getting upset. The will is very clear. The land goes to Suzanne and her children."

"How will she take care of it?" Fabrisse demanded.

"The boys will be back soon," Mama replied. "Until then I hope for help from all of you."

Uncle Fabrisse simply grunted and sat down and glowered at everyone.

Papa had always irritated his older brothers. He'd always been the adventurous one, and he had become far more successful than anyone in or around our village, probably because he took risks. Even in death it seemed he was not going to do what his family expected. As I look back on it now, I know that his behavior was unusual, but at the time I simply took my father's ways for granted. Uncle Fabrisse was always mad at him for one thing or another, and this will was another, if the final one, in a long line of angry episodes. The fact that he'd left his property to Mama did not surprise me. They had always made decisions together; Mama knew a lot about his business dealings and worked the land with him, so it seemed most logical. But I did not know then what I learned since. And I suppose, if I could choose, I might choose my happy ignorance of those days to the terrible knowledge I now possess.

That night, once I got into the bed I usually shared with Marguerite in the room behind the kitchen, I was sure I wouldn't be able to sleep. So I asked Mama if I could sleep with her in bed upstairs. I was nestled under the quilt, almost asleep, when I felt Mama sit up and heard her exclaim, "Fabrisse, just what are you doing?"

"Now, Suzanne," I heard my uncle reply, "this business of you taking over the land is ridiculous." I could hear him walking into the room. I started to move, but Mama kicked me so I'd be still.

"Why is it ridiculous?"

"Who is going to work it without Philippe here and both boys away?"

"They are only on a short trip," Mama answered. "We will manage until they return. I was thinking of hiring Pierre Arsen for a while."

"A boy like that? His father doesn't even own an inch of land."

"I know," Mama replied. "That is why I'm sure he'll be happy for the work."

The bed creaked as Uncle Fabrisse lowered himself onto it. "Suzanne, you will need a protector. A man who will manage your affairs and work the land. You mustn't worry. I will take care of you." He paused. "In every way."

"Fabrisse," my mama replied, her voice tight, "I will need a friend, many friends. But I assure you my sons and I can manage on our own!"

"But it's unheard of!" Fabrisse exclaimed, getting up. "It's *my* land."

"No, Fabrisse, it is mine. My sons will be back soon to go over all the papers and make sure everything is in order."

"Will they?" he said.

"What do you mean?"

"Will they be back soon? I'm not so sure of that, Suzanne. A letter might reach them telling them *not* to come home."

Mama threw the comforter off and leapt out of bed. "You wrote them and told them to come home, didn't you? Didn't you?"

"I did. And I could write them again. Suzanne, please, reconsider. Let us be friends."

My mother's voice was low and intense. "Leave this room, Fabrisse. I cannot believe you, Philippe's own brother, would behave this way to me. Leave or I'll scream and wake Bernadette."

"All right, Suzanne. I'm going," he said in a wheedling voice, suddenly afraid that Mama might make a fuss and wake my aunt.

When he was gone, Mama got back into bed. I could feel her trembling.

"Mama, what are we going to do?" I whispered.

"I will go to Father Bernard tomorrow and ask him to write Guillaime for me. I will tell him the exact words to use. Don't worry. The boys will come back before Fabrisse can do any harm. Now go to sleep, little Rose." She kissed me on the forehead and I snuggled up to her.

I suppose I should have been frightened at that point, but I wasn't. Uncle Fabrisse had always had an eye for Mama—she and Papa used to joke about it. It was just typical of my difficult uncle to try to bully Mama into giving over our land *and* sharing her bed. I was disgusted, but not totally surprised. Mama, however, was more than a match for him, and although I could see she was upset, I was confident that she would maneuver us through this. Perhaps all would have been well in the end, if unpleasant for a while, had events not taken another unexpected turn.

In the morning Mama hurried off to see Father Bernard, and that night she asked me to keep her company in case she should need my help with Uncle Fabrisse. I actually would have preferred to sleep with Marguerite, as I wasn't used to the idea that Mama might need my help. Papa had always been there for her, or my brothers. But I knew I couldn't say no, so I hid under the comforter and hoped Uncle Fabrisse would leave her alone. I had already fallen asleep when

Mama's voice so startled me I almost jerked up in bed and gave away my presence.

"Fabrisse, I want friendship and, yes, protection—but I will not give you my land." She paused. "Or anything else."

"Suzanne, you will be lonely. You'll be glad to have me look after your land. You'll be glad to have me share your bed. Please. Don't be so stubborn. Think of what is best for you, for Rose."

"I know what is best for us, Fabrisse. Now leave or I will call Bernadette."

Just then Aunt Bernadette threw open the bedroom door. "Fabrisse," she screamed, "get out of here!" I popped out from under the covers to get a better view. Then she turned to Mama. "You! You have put a spell on him. You've bewitched him. He's a good man and your husband is barely cold and you are scheming to get mine!"

She came at Mama and tried to scratch her face. Mama caught her hands and wrestled with her.

"Fabrisse, take her out of here," Mama ordered. Uncle Fabrisse caught hold of Aunt Bernadette and dragged her out of the room.

I leapt out of the bed and called after them, "It wasn't Mama. I heard everything. It was Uncle Fabrisse!"

Mama shut the door and began to pace back and forth. "How could he?" she exclaimed. "Your papa must be turning in his grave. Fabrisse should be our protector; instead he's a wolf. It's disgusting! Never mind, Rose," Mama continued. "I've got my eye on the little cottage at the edge of the village, owned by the Church. I'm sure Father Bernard will sell it to me; it's been empty now for years. It's cozy, just the right size for us. Until your brothers return, we'll be better off there.

It has a lovely garden, so we can grow our herbs, and we'll hire someone to look after the crops with us. We needn't stay here one extra minute if we don't want to!"

I had mixed feelings about Mama's idea. I felt she was right to be angry with my aunt and uncle—they were behaving terribly! And I was glad to see she wasn't afraid to move away so we could be free of their nasty attentions. On the other hand, I would miss being with Marguerite all the time. And I was nervous about a move, just because it was new and I *was* worried about how we would manage on our own. Still, with Papa gone I chose to put my faith in her good sense and not to worry her with unnecessary questions.

The next morning the whole family was in an uproar, arguing and accusing Mama.

Marguerite pulled me aside.

"Why did your mama make such a scene last night?" she asked. "Is she becoming unbalanced because of your papa's death?"

For a moment I could only stare at her.

"My mama did not make a scene," I said, my temper getting the better of me. "Your father came to her room and made advances."

Marguerite's face flushed red. "He did not!"

"Marguerite, I was under the covers. I heard everything." I paused a moment. "I'm sorry to have to tell you this."

She didn't reply, but simply glared at me and walked off. I couldn't tell if she believed me and was mad at her father or if she felt I was making the whole story up to protect Mama—but we'd always been honest with one another. I wasn't surprised she was upset, and I told myself that she would calm down and realize that none of it was *my* fault—or Mama's. As sorry as I was to be moving away from Marguerite, I felt quite differently about my other cousins. Jean, for instance, just a year older than me, was particularly nasty, growling at me about how we were stealing the land he always thought would be his.

The cottage Mama and I moved into was very different from our old house. It had only one floor, not two, and rather than separate bedrooms there was only one large room, which served as kitchen and bedroom. Still, once Mama's big four-poster bed sat in the rear of the room and our table was placed before the fire, our pots and pans were hung, and Mama's dried herbs filled the air with their scent, it was quite cozy.

We had a perfect view of the church at the bottom of the hill, and a lovely view of the chateau at the top of the hill. The village green was in the middle, with houses running along terraces from top to bottom.

M. Gaillac, his wife and their children, including Raymond, came to help us move, as well as Father Bernard and a few young lads from the village. Raymond was a year older than I and was M. Gaillac's eldest son. I thought he was very handsome—tall with big shoulders and blond hair and green-gray eyes. He was particularly kind that day. He brought us flowers he had gathered to help brighten the cottage. For once he didn't engage me in our usual banter but was sensitive to my mood. I was grateful to him for that. He reminded me of the way Papa behaved, always considering others' feelings. Uncle Fabrisse tried to get people in the village on his side, tried to get them to shame us into moving back and giving up the land, but few seemed to care about our family feud. Neighbors had too much respect for Mama and didn't want her angry at them when they or their children took sick.

After the move our lives took on an almost frantic quality. Mama had to oversee our many fields, as it was the harvest time for the hay. We worked all day, along with different neighbors who took turns helping. In return for their work, Mama paid them a percentage of the harvest. She also hired Pierre, whose father worked as a laborer for the count, to work for us full-time.

Pierre was a bit stupid and needed direction in everything, but he was strong, not at all lazy, and eager to please. I had to abide his disgusting habit of spitting constantly, and his clothes looked and smelled as if washing was done once a year, but Mama was pleased with his help. She reminded me that we didn't have to live with him; we just had to let him work our fields.

We had to transplant as many of her herbs as we could to our new garden and tend to them all. And almost every day someone needed Mama's help when there was an accident or a sickness. Each night we fell into bed exhausted and woke the next morning with too much work to do again.

As soon as the hay was harvested we had to weed the other crops, and then finish the sheep shearing before midsummer night. I couldn't wait for the midsummer night's festivities. I needed a break from work and I needed something to take my mind off missing Papa so much. I wanted to dance all night and even to visit with Marguerite. I hoped we would still be friends despite my uncle's animosity toward Mama.

But before any of that, the sheep had to be shorn. The entire village did that job together, so we had to see a lot of

Papa's family. They treated Mama and me badly, speaking just under their breaths, calling us thieves, saying we would ruin Papa's property, which was rightfully theirs anyway. They said we would manage it so badly that soon it would be worthless.

"Two women alone," Uncle Fabrisse muttered. "It's against nature."

And then Uncle Jacues went right up to Mama and said, "Now, Suzanne, this quarreling has gone on long enough. Our lands should be united once again. You cannot manage these huge holdings on your own. I have a proposal."

"Yes?" Mama said, a wary look in her eye.

"Your Rose will marry my Jean. It's a perfect match. It will bring the families together; you'll move back with us; and we'll put all this unpleasantness behind us."

My heart leapt into my throat.

"No, Jacues," Mama said. "It is not a suitable match for Rose. You know yourself how peevish Jean can be."

"Rose will tame him," Jacues replied.

Even he couldn't deny Jean's unpleasant character.

"She will do no such thing," Mama replied. "We are quite happy the way things are. And my sons will be back to give me the extra help I need."

I was so relieved, my knees almost buckled. Uncle Jacues marched off looking very angry, and soon the family was grumbling furiously, angrier than ever at us. But it would never have occurred to me then that their anger would become dangerous.

chapter three

Mama decided that midsummer day would be spent in our garden, weeding and tending the herbs and plants and gathering those ready for cutting. Father Bernard, who seemed to be constantly hovering around us wherever we went, turned up again.

"Can I help, Suzanne?" he asked.

"Well, Father, if you are looking for extra work I won't say no," Mama replied. "This row badly needs weeding."

Father Bernard moved his pinched mouth in a peculiar way, which I suppose was meant to be a smile, and squinted at us over his hooked nose. He bent down in the dirt and gingerly began to pluck at the weeds.

"It must be hard for you, Suzanne," he said, "without your dear Philippe."

At the mention of my father's name I suddenly started to cry. I had become inexplicably emotional since Easter, a few months earlier—one minute elated over nothing, the next minute miserable. I never knew when a different mood would hit me. Mama said it was because I was becoming a young woman and that often played tricks on our bodies—she had seen it in other young women my age. Sometimes I didn't think of Papa for days, but other times I missed him so intensely I felt I would die. He had always shown me extra attention. He called me his little Rose and told me I was just like the flower I was named after—beautiful, dignified, but with the thorns of a fighter. I liked that. Actually, Mama was the real beauty. Even at her age she had all her teeth, her hair was black as a raven's, her eyes were the color of the sky, her skin was almost a pure white. I did look very much like her, and I was tall and slim like her as well, but it wasn't all put together in the way it was with her. Papa used to say that when I grew up I would be the most beautiful girl in the entire region—besides Mama.

"Of course it is hard, Father," Mama replied, "and his family isn't making it any easier on us. They know they have no case against me or they would have taken this whole matter before the courts. So why do they persist in trying to make us miserable?"

"Well, Suzanne, you must see it from their perspective. Here you are, a woman from another village, no family property here at all, and Philippe goes and leaves you what has been in their family for generations. Of course they are bitter." He paused for a minute. "You and Rose need a protector, Suzanne."

"That would be nice, Father." Mama smiled. "And who would you suggest?"

"It could be me," he answered, so quietly I barely heard him. "I could keep Fabrisse away from you—and don't forget how I helped you by writing that letter to your sons."

"But of course, Father, you already are my protector," Mama answered, her face flushing, although at first I didn't understand why. "You protect my soul from danger. And how could I forget the service you did me when you wrote Arnaud and Guillaime?"

"You know," Father Bernard muttered, "some priests *do* still marry. Well, informally, that is."

Mama's face grew quite red. I was shocked at what he was suggesting!

She said, in a very low voice, "I will not be the Church's mistress, Father. I am ashamed of you that you should ask it of me. You should be my protector with no payment expected."

He stood up, his lanky form towering over her as she crouched by her plants.

"I did not expect payment," he declared. "You insult me, Madame. I was expressing love. But perhaps you have a devil inside you, preventing you from loving your Church!"

"I love my Church, Father," Mama said, also standing. "It is *you* I do not love! Now please go and let us forget this entire unfortunate episode."

"Yes," Father Bernard agreed, his face pale, his beady eyes glaring at us both, "let us try to forget it."

And he stomped off. Before he had gone too far, I could see Mama's face get redder and redder. I couldn't tell whether she was angry or about to cry, when suddenly, to my surprise, she burst out laughing. Unfortunately it carried all the way to Father Bernard's ears. He swung around to see her in a fit of hysterical laughter. Nothing about it seemed to strike him as humorous. His face became even paler, and he glowered at us both for a moment before he twisted around and continued on his way. The thought of Mama as the priest's mistress struck me as very funny too suddenly, and I joined her in laughter. We were both sitting on the ground, tears falling down our faces from laughing so hard, when my cousin Christoph ran over to us.

"Please, Aunt Suzanne, Mama has taken very ill. Will you come?"

"Why should you, Mama?" I asked. "After she almost threw us out of her house, blaming Uncle Fabrisse's advances on you!"

"I must try to help her, Rose," Mama admonished me. "Now come along. What are her symptoms, Christoph?"

"As you know, everyone in the household has had an illness," Christoph said. "Fever, coughing, sneezing—but we have all gotten better quickly. But Mama is having trouble breathing now. She coughs until her chest hurts, and her fever is very high."

Mama went into the house and gathered some herbs and some liquid potions. Then we accompanied Christoph to our old home. Aunt Bernadette was in her bed in her room on the second floor. She did not look well. Her breathing was very shallow and weak, her fever very high.

"Why didn't someone call me sooner?" Mama demanded. She glared at Uncle Fabrisse.

"She didn't want you," he replied. "She says you are in league with the devil."

Mama snorted and shook her head. "She is very ill. You should have called me sooner. Has she had any willow bark tea?"

"She wouldn't take anything," Uncle Fabrisse muttered.

"You must get her to drink this tea to help bring down the fever," Mama ordered. "And I want you to give her three drops of this extract in her wine, morning, midday and night. It should calm the cough and help her to rest. And try to get her to eat garlic, because the illness is taking over her body and it needs to be fought. Also, I want you to make her a hot mustard poultice and put it on her chest." Mama went over all her instructions again and promised to return at sunset to see how Aunt Bernadette was faring.

As we walked back to our cottage, Mama looked grim.

"Will she die?" I asked.

"I think so," Mama replied. "She is near death now. The illness is in her chest, filling it with phlegm, which will choke her. The mixture I gave them will help ease her cough and let her rest. It is the only hope she has." Mama kicked at a rock. "Stupid woman! Was her hatred for me so strong she would rather die than ask for my help? Had they called me even yesterday I might have been able to coax the illness out of her."

"You can coax illness out of just about anyone," I replied. She could hear the pride in my voice.

Mama ruffled my hair. "Maybe if she can rest, her body will be able to heal itself. That's all we can hope for."

I felt bad, but I was determined to go to the midsummer night celebrations despite my aunt's illness. I was being pig-headed, I know that now, yet I was so angry at her and at my uncle that I couldn't forgive them, even when I knew how ill Aunt Bernadette was. Marguerite had barely spoken to me when we were there. I felt my presence would get her more agitated, if anything. And I must admit, I was hoping for a dance with Raymond.

When I arrived at the village green, everyone was already dancing in the shadow of a huge bonfire. The musicians were in fine form, and I could see all the young people dancing together in a circle, including Raymond. He stood out taller than the rest. I was hurrying over to them when a strong hand gripped my wrist and held me. It was Pierre, our hired man.

"Rose," he said, "I must talk to you."

"You *are* talking to me, Pierre," I answered.

"No, listen."

"I *am* listening," I teased.

"Rose, I see you and your mama struggling and working so hard and I can't help but think—"

"You've been *thinking*, Pierre!" I exclaimed. "Heavens."

"Rose!" he replied. "I am asking you to marry me!"

I just stood there. Dumbfounded. And then I laughed.

His face got all red and he looked very angry. "Don't you laugh at me!"

"No, I'm not! Well, I mean, Pierre, it's ridiculous." And then *I* got angry. "How dare you?"

"Your father is dead, Rose. Your mother and you are without a man to take care of you."

"My brothers are coming home soon, and my mother and I are just fine with your help, Pierre," I said, softening a bit, seeing that he was sincere. "But it isn't right for you to propose to me like this."

"You should be glad of it, Rose. You can't afford to be so proud."

"Pierre, I'm not being proud—oh, never mind! My mother would never allow me to marry you anyway. Be sensible and enjoy the evening. I'm going to dance."

I ran off to join the group, feeling so confused, so angry, so shocked. What made Pierre think he could simply walk up to me and propose? He had no land to offer, only himself. Now, that would be enough for me if I loved him, but he had made no effort to be nice to me, to get to know me, to try to get me to love him. It seemed that I was supposed to be grateful for his offer of protection. If both Mama and I had accepted our marriage proposals, imagine our household— me, Mama, Father Bernard and Pierre! I was beginning to realize that Papa's death didn't just mean missing Papa.

When I reached the circle of dancers, Raymond caught my hand and pulled me along. His grip was strong and warm, and I smiled at him as I spun around.

Suddenly, though, the music faltered and people slowed their dancing. I quickly saw the reason. Through the smoke and the flames of the bonfire I saw four strangers ride into view. Their leader was a man cloaked in black, a high black hat on his head, riding a tall white mare. He looked at us with such revulsion and disdain that soon the bagpipes died and the village folk stopped their revelry. Everyone stared. Who would be traveling at such an hour? Who could this man be?

When all were quiet, he called from his horse. "I am Monsieur de Lancre, judge, with full powers bestowed on me by your King Henry the Fourth and by the parliament in Montpellier. I command you all to be at the village square tomorrow at the lunch hour, where I will make my announcements. Someone take me to your priest."

Father Bernard was not celebrating with us, of course. He considered midsummer night's festivities un-Christian and would have nothing to do with them.

Pierre ran forward with a lighted rush and led the judge's horse down the path toward the church. A chill ran through me as they passed by. I bid a quick farewell to Raymond then and turned to hurry toward my old house to tell Mama about his arrival.

But when I got there I didn't get the chance. I discovered that my aunt had just died. And my uncle was ranting at Mama.

"It's all your fault. She was all right until she drank that potion. Then she went to sleep and never woke up."

"She was dying," Mama replied. "All that potion did was help ease her cough. The rest was in God's hands."

"God!" Uncle Fabrisse exploded. "What would you know of Him? It's the devil you're in league with. You've killed my wife! Now get out of our house!"

"Fabrisse," Mama said calmly, "I know you are grieving the loss of Bernadette and that you don't mean what you say." With that she took my hand and we walked quickly home by the light of the moon. I didn't tell Mama about Pierre or M. de Lancre. She had enough to worry about. Besides, how could I have imagined the nightmare that this judge was bringing with him?

chapter four

After the midday meal, the entire village met in the square, with much grumbling and complaining. It meant almost everyone had to come in from the fields. Who was this judge and what did he want? I wondered secretly if it had anything to do with Mama's lands. Had Uncle made a complaint? What the judge actually said took me completely by surprise.

"All people," he declared, "that would bring in any complaint against any woman for a witch must do so now or fear for their own salvation."

Father Bernard stood beside him. "Excommunication from the Church," Father Bernard shouted, "will be the punishment for anyone who does not tell us who among our villagers are witches, for these women have made pacts with the devil and must be rooted out of our society. M. de Lancre and I will wait in the church for you to come and name those you suspect. And never fear. We will find them and we will defeat the devil here."

I felt like laughing, but of course I didn't want to draw attention to myself, so I controlled the impulse. Witches? Here? It was ridiculous! After all, everyone in our village knew everyone else so well—what they did, who they did it with. Surely we would have noticed if women were acting strangely.

People began to drift away from the square, breaking off into little groups, murmuring to each other, some even eyeing others as if they were wondering if their neighbors *could* be witches. As Mama and I walked past Mme Befayt, she made the sign of the cross and muttered something to her husband about potions. Others scurried off, looking at the ground, as if afraid they would be accused. I was confused by everyone's behavior. Why didn't they just laugh about it? Surely they all realized how ridiculous the entire idea was!

Mama grabbed my hand tightly and we walked back to our cottage instead of the fields.

"I have heard of this man from your dear father," she said to me, her voice low. "Your father traveled to Montpellier just after this witch-hunter had been there. A hundred women were burned for being witches, and people wept as they told your father of the burnings. Many lost wives and mothers and neighbors. I am very much afraid," she added, and her voice trembled.

"Mama!" I remonstrated. "Don't be foolish. I am sure there are no witches here. Well, there is Madame Trembley, who is always cursing those who won't feed her when she begs, but she is the *only* one who could be accused and everyone knows her curses are nonsense and are made out of anger. Witches!" And I actually giggled. "I suppose," I continued, "that there was a large group of them practicing witchcraft in Montpellier and they had to be stopped. But we have nothing to worry about here."

"Rose," Mama said, "you don't understand. The women who were burned in Montpellier were no more witches than you or I. They were just ordinary women."

"How do you know that?"

"Your papa told me. He knew some of their families—he had known some of them!"

"Maybe they fooled him," I suggested. "Witches can do that."

"They were *not* witches," Mama said, beginning to sound annoyed. "They were accused by people who had grudges against them. They were brought to trial. Then they were tortured until they admitted they were witches and tortured further until they named other so-called witches. They named their own friends and neighbors. Some even named members of their own family."

A nasty chill ran up my spine. Falsely accusing your own family? How could that happen?

"We must get away until the witch-hunter has gone," Mama said, pulling me down the path that led to our cottage. "I don't trust him. And I don't trust Father Bernard."

"Father Bernard?" I asked. "Why ever not?"

"Don't you remember how angry he became when I spurned his advances? And we have other enemies now. I don't like it. We must leave. Tonight. After dark we will sneak away. We will find Arnaud and Guillaime and stay with them until this has all passed over."

"But we can't, Mama!" I objected. "What about our fields? We still have the grains to harvest. We can't leave now! And what will my brothers do without the harvest to sell? How will we live? We will all starve together."

By this time we were home in our garden.

"We will not starve," she said. "I will have Arnaud write a letter for us, asking Pierre and others to do the harvest for a percentage of the gross. They will do that and send us the money."

My stomach was all in a twist. Mama, who was always calm, even in the worst crisis, now seemed to be making no sense at all.

"Mama," I pleaded, "be reasonable." Another terrible thought struck me. "People will say we ran away *because* we are witches. The judge will pass sentence on us in our absence and take away everything. We must stay. No one will accuse you of anything—except saving half the village from sickness or death at one time or another."

"No, I don't care what you say—we must leave," Mama insisted. "I can feel it in my bones. No good will come of this and I don't want to be here. Your father told me terrible stories. He told me that these judges feel only a confession given under torture is a true confession. That's what he said. Now go inside and put as much as you can carry into a pack. Do mine as well. I shall stay out here tending the garden so that all looks normal."

It was clear that Mama would not be reasoned with, so I hurried inside and followed her instructions even though I thought it was sheer madness. Now, of course, I realize that she was not crazy but was doing as she always did—she looked at the situation and quickly took action. At the time her actions seemed almost mad to me because I couldn't really grasp what was going on. And the thought that she was behaving in what *I* thought was a crazy way caused me to become nervous and scared and confused all at once. I found that my hands trembled as I chose clothes and foodstuffs for our journey. I had this terrible feeling, similar to the terror I'd felt when Papa died, that in one moment everything had changed and would never be the same again. After all, even when we returned, would we be welcomed back by our neighbors? Or would they forever be suspicious of us for running away? Wouldn't it just strengthen Uncle Fabrisse's case against us? By the time we returned he would have everyone on his side. And anyway, who would be accused? I couldn't imagine anyone accusing their neighbors or their friends. How could they?

"Your uncle Fabrisse has been into the church," Mama muttered to me when I joined her in the garden. "And the doctor from the chateau. And Pierre. What is Pierre doing there? Why isn't he working the fields? And Madame Trembley has been taken to the church by those three men who accompanied the judge."

"Mama, I don't want to go," I said.

"My dear Rose, neither do I," she replied. "But when that man entered our village, our choices about everything changed." She took my hands in hers. "Rose," she said, "you don't realize that things are not the way you think them to be." She sighed. "I don't know how to explain this to you, or if you'll understand, but you must try. When Papa met me, I was already a respected healer in my village. He knew he was marrying a woman with opinions and strength. He loved me for it. But many others do not see me that way."

I tried to object. "Everyone loves you, Mama!"

"No, flower," That was Mama's pet name for me. "The doctor doesn't. He hates me. He fears the fact that I am better at his job than he is. Your uncle doesn't. He is jealous of our land. And even some of our neighbors fear me—they wonder how I can cure so well; they make the sign of the cross as I leave their homes. Had this man, this witch-hunter, not come here, these feelings would have stayed buried, harmless. But now I fear that they will have an outlet, and that means danger for us. Papa and I have always been a little different, and you've grown up accepting that—the way everyone is different. But some differences can hurt you. I hope," she added, "that fleeing tonight is soon enough—but I have a feeling that if we tried now and they saw, us we would be stopped."

Mama's words swam in my head and I tried to make sense of them. Had I misunderstood everything around me? And if so, how could I understand anything now? I was so confused I couldn't think, so I tried to put it all out of my mind as I bent over the weeds. It was hot that day, I remember, and the sky was filled with those lovely fluffy clouds I like so much and the mountains shimmered in the distance. I loved our village. I had never left it, and I didn't want to leave! I could feel tears trickling down my face as I worked, mingling with the sweat.

Finally it was time for the evening meal.

"Is everything packed?" Mama asked as we ate a plain meal of bread and cheese.

I nodded.

"Good. We will wait until well into the hour of the first sleep. The moon will be bright tonight."

I could see that she would not waver in her resolve, so I busied myself by helping her mix some fresh powders and label them with the correct symbols. Then we sat by the fire, not exchanging words, each sunk in our own thoughts. I had never really wanted to travel. Father used to travel quite a lot, selling our harvest, going to fairs, trading and bartering, and Mama traveled to visit those who needed her. When Guillaime turned sixteen, Father began to take him on his trips, until finally Guillaime did most of the traveling, and he soon had Arnaud trailing after him. I always stayed home and minded things for them here. Had Father offered me the chance to go with him, I would have refused, and even when Mama wanted my company to go to a nearby village I declined. The thought of bandits and thieves on the open road terrified me; the thought of the noise and rush of big towns and cities dismayed me. How would I live without my beautiful mountains or the smell of Mama's garden full of fresh herbs, or without working the land? I didn't seem to have a choice in the matter. If Mama was right about all this, I would have to find pleasure in other things.

I suppose I must have dozed off by the fire, for I awoke to Mama gently shaking me. The fire was out completely, and she was holding my pack in her hand. Hers was already on her back.

"It's time, flower."

I took the pack, put it on and followed her to the door. I was too sleepy even to take one last look. I simply staggered after her out into the night. All was quiet, but the moon gave off a good light and it wasn't difficult to follow the road. We were the last cottage, so we didn't have to worry about waking the dogs or the animals in our neighbor's yards as we went past. We hurried down the path, then stopped for a moment as we neared the church. Mama looked around and then motioned for me to follow. It seemed that the church was deserted. Still, I noticed that Mama picked up her pace until we were almost running as we passed it. Suddenly the church doors were flung open and Father Bernard screamed, "Stop, witch!" From the trees across the road a dreadful yelling began as people ran out from behind them and out of the church.

"Ah, dear God, have mercy on me and my child," Mama cried as she was gripped by two of M. de Lancre's men.

"Invoke your true god," M. de Lancre's voice boomed, deep and sonorous. "Invoke your true helpmeet, the devil."

I tried to make out who the other men were. Uncle Fabrisse, Jean, Pierre, all three of M. de Lancre's men and three others that I knew from the village, Brunissende and his two grown sons. They pulled Mama into the church. Almost as an afterthought, Father Bernard turned to look at me and said, "Bring her as well. Make her watch." And they grabbed me and dragged me in with them.

How shall I tell what happened next? In some ways it is still unclear—my fear and confusion were so great I could barely comprehend *what* was happening. And as events unfolded, my fear heightened to such an extent that for much of the time I was in a kind of swoon, punctured only by terror and pain. But it was the humiliation we suffered that was the worst part—worse than any pain.

M. de Lancre's men grabbed Mama and stripped her clothes off. She fought them, screaming, until one of them hit her so hard across the face she was stunned and stopped fighting.

Father Bernard stared at my mother's body with unabashed lust—as did the other men. I was horrified, so angry I couldn't control myself.

"Have you no shame?" I cried to them all. "Father, can you call this a Christian undertaking?"

He turned his beady eyes on me and said, in a low voice, "We'll see who laughs now, Rose."

They tied her to a long table and, by the light of the rushes, took a sharp razor and began to shave her. I thought they meant to cut her to bits and I screamed and screamed and struggled with Pierre and Jean, who were holding me, until Jean hit me too, right across the jaw. My head swam and I felt so sick I could no longer fight—but I looked on, my sight often clouded over by the tearing produced by the blow I had received. It took them a long time to shave Mama's entire body. They forced her to stand in the light of the rushes. Mama was very modest—even at night she slept with her shift on. To strip her naked and shave her—it was too horrible. I shook from head to foot with fear and anger and shame. One of M. de Lancre's men approached Mama with a long, pointed instrument.

"This is my witch pricker," M. de Lancre announced. "He will search for the devil's mark."

"Who accuses me?" Mama screamed. "What am I accused of?"

I was surprised to hear Mama speak, thinking she would be humiliated into silence. But she would not let them defeat her so easily.

"Many accuse you, Madame," M. de Lancre replied, his face hovering over hers. His thick black eyebrows furrowed together, his full lips leered. "Many."

The witch pricker then began to scrutinize Mama's body, his hands moving over her skin as his eyes peered closely at every inch of her. When he found a mole or a beauty mark, he stabbed it with the long needle. Each time she was stabbed, blood spurted and Mama screamed. Finally, after what seemed an eternity of blood and agony, and my screams mixed with hers, the witch pricker stood and declared, "She bled and she cried out. Proof is clear only when the marks do not bleed, or she does not cry out."

So then I thought, They will have to let her go. She has passed their miserable test.

Instead, M. de Lancre announced, "Then she must confess. And the confession must be made under torture to be a true confession."

"No," Mama gasped, her voice almost strangled by the horror of what she'd just heard.

"No!" I echoed.

They threw her clothes at her and let her dress. She could barely get her clothes back on, her hands shook so hard. Once dressed, she looked back at me with the most pitiable gaze as they dragged her past me and out of the church.

I called to her and reached for her, but Pierre and Jean held me strong in their grip.

"Where are they taking her?" I sobbed.

"To the chateau," Pierre replied. "They will hold her in the cellar there."

"But why? And why are you helping them?" I said to him. "She was only good to you."

"No," he snorted, "she bewitched you so that you laughed at me when I asked you to marry me. Who knows but that she hasn't pulled you into her coven as well," he added, a look on his face of both fear and fascination. "Perhaps soon it will be your turn for the witch pricker."

I shook myself loose from him and Jean.

"Go home now," Jean said. "And if you still believe in God, pray to him your mother confesses."

I turned and ran to our cottage. It was cold, as it often was at night—even at midsummer—and I hadn't the energy to restart the fire. I huddled under the goose quilt in Mama's big bed, and I shook and shook until I fell into some kind of stupor and only came out of it when the first cock crowed.

chapter five

When I awoke the next morning, I realized just how alone I was. Who could I look to for help? Father Bernard had turned against us with all the vengeance of a spurned lover. My father's family had also turned against us, as had even our paid help, Pierre. But surely our friends and neighbors would do something. I would simply go from house to house and ask everyone to go to M. de Lancre and speak on Mama's behalf. He would see then that everyone in our village loved her; he would understand that she was innocent.

Quickly I washed myself and plaited my hair. The first house I went to was the Aurilhacs'. They had five children and all of them had needed Mama's help at one time or another. The oldest was twelve. The children were in the yard feeding the animals; their mother was milking the goat. I ran up to her.

"Madame, Madame, you must help me. My poor mama has been taken to the chateau, accused of being a witch."

"I know that," she replied, not even looking at me. "Jean was by here even earlier telling everyone that she is accused."

"Madame, please, go to this judge. You and Monsieur Aurilhac. Tell him how Mama has helped you. Tell him how she saved little Maurice when he ate those mushrooms and how she brought all your children into the world and—"

"That's enough, child," Mme Aurilhac interrupted. "I can tell him nothing," she muttered, still not meeting my eyes.

"I don't understand," I said. "Why can't you speak to him?"

"Because," she said fiercely, "I have five children who need their mother! And if I speak for your mama, the judge will think I am part of her coven. He'll arrest me. I must keep out of sight. That is my best chance."

"No!" I exclaimed. "If you go together, all the people, he'll see he's made a mistake."

"I can't help what others will do," she said. "But I won't go. Now you run along, Rose. I don't want you seen here talking to me." She looked around to make sure no one had noticed me come into her yard.

I didn't move.

"Go on."

I was frozen to the spot. I simply couldn't believe that this woman wouldn't lift a finger to help us.

"Go on!" she almost screamed.

I turned and ran. I hurried up the road and threw open the gate of the Befayts' house, but before I was even two steps into the yard M. Befayt ran over to me and yelled, "Out of here, out!"

"Monsieur," I cried, "Mama needs help."

"Out! Out!" he yelled, as if I were some wild dog.

I fled, and at each house the same scene was repeated. The nicer ones talked and explained, the others just screamed at me to be gone. Finally I reached my old home and saw my cousin Marguerite in her yard. I didn't dare go in. I was panting from running, and tears were falling down my cheeks. I called to her. "Marguerite, Marguerite, come over here."

Slowly she came over to the hedge that surrounded the property. "Of course you know what has happened to Mama," I said.

She nodded.

"Can't you talk to your father? Is he the one accusing her? Can't you make him see reason?"

For a moment Marguerite didn't answer. Finally, eyes downcast, she replied, "I don't know what to believe anymore."

"What do you mean?" I exclaimed. "Surely you can't believe what your father says. He's just angry."

"And why is he angry?" Marguerite answered, her eyes flashing. "Because my mother died after drinking one of your mother's potions."

"Marguerite, you can't mean what you're saying," I argued. "You must stop and think. Your mother was dying, that was clear to everyone. Mama couldn't stop it. And what about the time years ago when she saved your mother after your mother had fallen on a rake and punctured her leg and the bleeding wouldn't stop? Mama stopped the bleeding and healed the wound."

"Maybe she wasn't a slave of the devil *then*," Marguerite answered.

We had been best friends all our lives and now she

believed Mama was in league with the devil. I became so infuriated I could not control myself.

"Why, you!" And I slapped her, right across the face. Marguerite immediately started to cry and ran screaming to the house for her brothers. I didn't wait for them but hurried on my way, tears stinging my eyes as well, but now too angry to cry. Marguerite falling for these lies—it was beyond belief.

Just as I was nearing the last house in the village, Raymond moved in front of me on the road and blocked my path. I braced myself for more accusations and malicious thoughts.

"Rose," he said, "I've heard what has happened."

"So?" I replied.

"So I'm very sorry," he said. "Your mother brought me into this world, as she did all of my friends, and she took good care of my sister, Justine, when she was so sick. I'm sure there must be some mistake."

I was so relieved to hear someone speak in a friendly tone, my knees almost gave way beneath me.

"Are you all right?" he asked.

"No," I answered, all my anger and fear returning, "how could I be all right? Last night they did the most dreadful things to Mama..." And I stopped for a moment as the picture of what they had done came back to me so clearly I could barely speak. "They hurt her and they mean to hurt her more. How could I be all right? I'm frightened. I've been to every house in the village and no one will stand by her. I can't believe they can all turn against her like this."

"Everyone is afraid for themselves," Raymond replied. "Everyone is afraid it will be them next."

"I need someone who won't be afraid," I said. "Someone who can stand up to that judge." And then an idea came to me. "The countess! Mama saved her life. And her baby's. Surely *she* will intervene and send that horrid man away!"

Raymond looked at his feet as if reluctant to say what was on his mind.

"What is it?" I asked. "Do you think she will help me?"

"It may not be in her power to do so," Raymond said quietly. "As you know, I have traveled with my father to sell our crops and buy supplies, and I have heard that even the nobility is under the rule of those witch-hunting judges. The judge has authority from the parliament in Montpellier. What if the countess stands by your mother and is then accused herself of being an accomplice?"

"But is there no other law than him?" I cried. "No lawyer for Mama, no defense, nothing?"

"I believe his authority is supreme," Raymond replied, "just like the courts of the Inquisition. He is as powerful and is aided by the Church."

I looked up into his green-gray eyes and saw such kindness there that I wanted to throw myself into his arms and weep. Instead I said, "Thank you, Raymond. You are the only person who has said a friendly word to me since this began. Thank you." I moved around him and followed the road up the hill to the chateau. The countess was my only hope, and I at least had to try to gain her help.

When I reached the chateau I went directly to the kitchen entrance and asked one of the kitchen helpers to fetch Sylvie, the countess's maid. Eventually Sylvie came to the door.

"Can I see your master and your mistress?" I blurted out, assuming she knew what had happened to my mama. "I must plead with them for my mother's release."

Sylvie looked at me with a great deal of sympathy. "Your poor mama. They dragged her here in the middle of the night and put her in one of the cold cellar rooms. I could hear her weeping."

"Did you see her?" I asked. "*Can* you see her?"

Sylvie shook her head. "We've all been told to stay away from her, and one of those men who came with this Judge de Lancre sits outside her door. The judge has demanded lodging here for him and his men."

"Sylvie," I pleaded, "Mama saved your mistress's life. You know that is true. Please, please let me talk to your mistress."

"I'll see what I can do," Sylvie agreed. "You wait here."

I was allowed into the kitchen and given a cup of broth by one of the kitchen cooks. I sipped it and tried to gather my strength for the meeting and prayed to God to soften the countess's heart so she would at least see me, perhaps listen to me.

Sylvie came back, beaming. "She'll see you. The count is in bed, feeling unwell, but the countess will see you."

I was led to her room. This time she was sitting up in the bed, the baby in a cradle next to her fast asleep. The countess was very pretty and also very young—I had not realized how young when I had helped Mama. She had blond hair and large brown eyes and was plump. Her cheeks were rosy. She smiled at me. "Hello. You are called Rose, I believe."

"Yes, my lady."

"This is a terrible business, Rose."

"Yes, my lady."

"You wanted to speak to me?"

"Yes, my lady, please." I paused for a moment to gather my thoughts. What could I say to convince the countess? I had to find the right words. "Mama is innocent of all charges of witchcraft. I should know. I am with her every minute of the day. All she does is help people, my lady, people like yourself." Then I looked her right in her eyes. "My lady, my mother saved your life *and* the life of your child. You both would have died without her help. Now she has been falsely accused. Only you and your husband can save her. The witch-hunter will believe you. You must make him let her go." I paused again. "My lady, they are going to *torture* her."

Just then the door swung open and in stalked the countess's doctor.

"Well, well, well, if it isn't the witch's daughter. One of the servants said she was having an audience with you, my lady. I had to see for myself."

"She is not a witch," I screamed before I could stop myself.

"Is she not?" he replied. "And yet I, with all my skill, could not help the poor countess here, but your mother, a *woman*, with no training in medicine, an uneducated *woman*, saved her life. How can one explain that? There is only one way. Witchcraft. She had made a pact with the devil and she had powers none of us could understand."

Much to my surprise I found myself answering him.

"If she had made a pact with the devil," I responded, "why would she use her powers for good? Why would she save the life of the countess and her baby? Wouldn't the devil want them dead?"

To this day I do not know what prompted me to speak out this way to the doctor—I can only say that I forgot all about respect for my betters and could think only of saving my mother.

"Yes," agreed the countess, "this girl is quite right. Her mother did not harm us. Quite the opposite. It was *you*," the countess said to the doctor, "who could not help us."

My hopes began to rise. Perhaps I had an ally here. Perhaps she would stand up to all these men and make them let my mother go.

"Aha!" the doctor replied, his voice triumphant. "But *why* did she save you and the child? I'll tell you why. Because she plans to kill the baby and sacrifice it to the devil when it is a little older and fatter. And then she will ensnare you too—and that was her plan all along."

"That's just ridiculous," the countess replied, and yet she looked a little uncertain.

"If you think so," the doctor said, his voice smooth as honey, "why don't you go to Monsieur de Lancre and tell him he must free the woman? Tell him you personally can vouch for her. Let him become interested in *you* and why *you* are taking the part of a witch."

"But nothing has been proven against her," the countess objected.

"That is not true," the doctor replied. "According to one of the judge's own books on the subject, which I have read, the accusation itself is proof enough. All that is needed after that is the witch's own confession in order to make the burning legal. And this confession cannot be made freely, for that might be a way for the witch to escape torture. No, this confession must be made under torture. There will be two levels of torture. The first will extract her confession. The second will force her to name the other witches in her coven."

"Then you will force her to name innocent people," I exclaimed, "for there is no coven. Madame," I pleaded, "you must stop this now before Mama and our whole village are destroyed."

The countess looked very troubled.

"I will talk to the count," she said to me.

"I understand he is not well," I answered. "If Mama were not in one of your old cellars she could help him."

"The way she helped your aunt?" The doctor scoffed. "That won't be necessary. *I* will help him. I will bleed him with leeches in a few moments."

"That will only weaken him," I argued. "Mama never does that."

"She is an idiot village woman," the doctor said to the countess, "who cannot read or write or claim an education."

"That's not true," I objected. "She was taught everything by a wise woman who knew everything about healing and herbs and potions—"

"Potions!" the doctor interrupted. "There, you see!"

"Enough of this!" the countess exclaimed. "I will speak of this with my husband. In the meantime, I see no reason why the child cannot visit her mother for a few moments. Sylvie"—Sylvie had been standing quietly by the door throughout this conversation—"take this child to her mother and tell the guard I insist they be allowed to speak. Rose, I will send Sylvie to you when I have spoken to my husband. Come here."

I went up to her and she beckoned me closer. Then she whispered in my ear so the doctor couldn't hear. "I will help if I can. But I am frightened for me and for my baby. I do not know if there is *anything* I can do. I promise I will try, though. Now pretend to look angry."

I did not quite understand, but I pretended anger and stalked off. As I was leaving I heard her say to the doctor, "I told her that her mother would *never* get her hands on my baby—*if* she really is a witch. *And* I am not yet convinced, Doctor."

"You will be, Madame. You will be soon," I heard him answer as I followed Sylvie to the chateau cellar.

chapter six

I was no longer interested in the sumptuous surroundings of the chateau, and as I followed Sylvie I hardly saw anything except her skirt in front of me. Once we reached the lower level, however, I looked around intently because even then I began to wonder if there wasn't a way I could help Mama escape. The stone ceiling was low and arched, and the main passageway, also made out of huge blocks of stone, had many storerooms and workrooms leading off it. It was very cold and I shivered as we walked. Soon we reached a closed door. One of M. de Lancre's men sat on a stool just outside it. He was a small man, bald, with red cheeks, and he smiled at us as we approached.

"You may not see the witch," he said cheerfully.

"She's my mother, she's not a witch," I exclaimed.

At that he looked even jollier as he eyed me. "Well, perhaps you will join her soon."

I could see that he was thoroughly enjoying himself, and that made my skin crawl.

"The countess has ordered that the child be allowed to see her mama. Open the door this moment," Sylvie commanded.

"I don't care what the countess has ordered," the man said, smiling broadly. "My master the judge has not given me such orders."

Sylvie thought for a moment and then returned the smile. "Madame might suddenly have repairs to make on the rooms or company coming to visit and she wouldn't have room here. Would your master the judge like to sleep in the cold damp church or up here in comfort?" she retorted.

I had to give Sylvie credit for her quick thinking. After all, I was sure the countess hadn't the courage to actually throw them out. But it seemed enough that Sylvie should make the threat.

"Well, only for a brief moment, then." The man glowered, his smile fading quickly.

Sylvie opened the door for me and led me inside.

Mama was sitting on a camp bed attached to the stone wall, her skirts pulled around her for warmth. Her face was pale and her lips slightly blue from cold. Dried spots of blood stained her dress. Mama had always been so strong, so healthy—I had seen her ill only once with a fever, and I remember feeling at that time, "This cannot be my mama, the one I count on for everything." I felt the same thing as I stared at her: How could she be so transformed? Sylvie pushed me into the room and closed the door behind us.

"Oh, my dear child," Mama cried when she saw me. "They have not accused you too!"

"No, Mama," I reassured her as I ran to hold her, "they have not. I have been to the countess to plead for your release."

"And she talked so well, Madame," Sylvie said. "But that doctor is a mean soul and jealous of your skills, and he is a danger to you, no mistake."

"I know," said Mama as she held tight to me. "Everyone who has any grudge against me will see this as an excuse to be rid of me. And soon they will convince the entire village that it is my fault we had rains this year during the planting—and also my fault for the terrible snowstorm we had midwinter, when all those lambs were lost." Mama held my face in her hands. "My poor dear Rose. What will happen to you? This is my worry. Will they accuse you as well, because of me?"

Thinking of her accusers reminded me of the doctor's words, and I felt I had to warn her.

"Mama, the doctor said that they would torture you until you confessed and then more until you named others."

"I will never confess!" Mama vowed. "Never."

The door swung open.

"That's enough now," the jailer said, smiling. "Off you go."

Mama hugged me fiercely to her.

"Don't worry about me, child," she whispered. "Flee, if you can find a way. I am lost."

"No, Mama, do not say that," I whispered back. "I will not leave without you. I will not leave you here alone."

And then the man grabbed my arm and roughly pulled me out of the room.

"I will be back later," I declared, "with food for her and blankets."

"That will not be necessary," Sylvie said. "I will bring her both!" And she glared at the jailer and walked off.

"Perhaps," he cried after Sylvie, "you are one of her coven."

Sylvie ignored him and led me out through the kitchen door.

"Sylvie, I must thank you for taking me to your mistress and standing up to the guard at Mama's door. You are very brave."

"I am not brave," she said quietly. "But I know something about these witch-hunters—from my uncle who came to live with us after the Inquisition arrived in his town years ago. They took his wife, my aunt. And no one helped her. And then they took the rest of the women. So he taught me that hiding and being afraid don't work. Best to meet your enemies head-on! As soon as the mistress speaks to the master I will come and tell you of it," she assured me. "In the meantime, go home and work at your garden and let people see you have nothing to be ashamed of. Hold up your head." I thought I saw tears in her eyes then as she said, "Your mother is a good woman who saved the life of my mistress and her baby and I would hate to see harm come to her."

I hurried home, this time without encountering either Raymond or Marguerite. I couldn't help but wonder at finding such a good friend in Sylvie—and I realized how fortunate Mama and I were to have her on our side. Just as I was mulling over how I never could have predicted who would help me and who would turn against me, Pierre came running up the path and stopped me as I walked.

"Rose," he said, "I must speak with you."

"I have nothing to say to you," I snapped, remembering the feel of his hands on my arms as he held me while they tormented Mama. "Let me pass."

"But Rose, now that your mama is accused, you'll need a protector more than ever. And I've been thinking that although most will shun you, I will not. I will stand by you." He paused and spat. "I wish to propose to you again."

I couldn't believe he was saying this to me. "I consider you lower than the insects that crawl out after dark, Pierre. Marry you? You, my protector? Did you raise a hand to help my mama? No, you helped those vile men. Now let me pass or I won't answer for my actions!"

And truly, had he not stepped away I was ready to attack him with all the strength and fury inside me. In fact, I was a little sorry that he did move and I had no excuse to hit him.

"You'll regret this, Rose," he snarled. "You'll be sorry."

I walked past him, head held high, and hurried into our yard. I tended to our animals, our ewes and chickens, and then put on a soup with turnips, broad beans, bacon, cabbage, leeks and some of Mama's herbs. I hoped to send it to her when Sylvie came. As I made the soup, the encounter with Pierre played over and over again in my mind. Mixed with my fury at his audacity were feelings of doubt—I wondered if I had used my head properly. What would Mama have done? Perhaps I should have held my temper and tried not to make him more of an enemy than he already was. Perhaps I should even have pretended to consider his offer, and then maybe he would have helped me with Mama. I sighed. It was too late now. He was forever our enemy and I would have to live with that. And since he was my enemy, I regretted not hitting him while I had the opportunity.

The soup finished, I went outside, and rather than going directly to work on the garden, I sat on the bench just outside the kitchen door, shut my eyes and tilted my face up into the warm sun. Eyes closed, I listened for the footsteps of Sylvie, the only one who could bring me news of Mama. Instead of her light tread I detected a heavier one moving quickly up the path of our cottage, and my eyes flew open to see Raymond hurrying toward me.

"Raymond?" I said, not quite knowing what on earth he was doing there.

He stopped in front of the bench and took a deep breath before he spoke. "Rose, I have heard some very bad news. I've come to tell you that you must leave here immediately."

"Is it Mama?" I said, hardly daring to hear the answer.

"No, it is you," he replied. "Pierre has now accused you to Monsieur de Lancre."

My heart sank and I felt cold, even with the sun still hot on me. I had indeed made a dangerous enemy.

"How do you know?" I asked.

"I saw him hurrying to the chateau as he passed our house, so I ran out and stopped him and asked him why he was going there. He boasted to me that he was helping Father Bernard discover all the witches who lived here and that he was now convinced you are one of them."

"But how can he accuse me?" I demanded as I rose

from the bench. "Doesn't he need witnesses or proof of *any* kind?"

"All he needs to do is accuse you," Raymond stated. "The judge will provide proof in the form of a confession from you."

"You mean by putting me to the torture?" I asked, and I knew the answer before he replied.

"Yes," he said.

"I cannot run away," I argued. "I must stay and try to help Mama."

"What help will you be to her when she sees you imprisoned and has to watch you tortured?" Raymond asked.

Of course I didn't have an answer for him. But I did have another question. "And even if I were to try to escape, just how could I accomplish this? Mama and I tried last night and we were caught. Even if I managed to flee into the forests, they could easily overtake me on horseback."

"That occurred to me as well," Raymond agreed, "but I had an idea on my way here. Our family has a hut, up on the mountain where we have our high pastures for our sheep. No one is using it now, as Father has us all hunting and fishing while the weather is fine, and the sheep are grazing on a lower pasture. If you could get up to it, no one would think to look for you there—they would assume you were on the road to Marseilles to find your brothers, or going southwest perhaps, to Spain."

I thought about the idea for a moment and it seemed sensible. What I liked most about it, though, was that I would not have to flee the area and leave Mama behind. "I would be close enough to come down at night and try to visit Mama," I said.

"That would be a very dangerous undertaking," Raymond warned.

Just as I was about to tell him that, dangerous or not, I would attempt it, I saw Sylvie running down the road toward us. I flew down the path and met her.

"Well, Sylvie, what is the news?"

Her face was flushed from running, and she gasped for breath.

"The news is bad," she said. "Madame talked to the master and he agreed to help—but in this way only. He has decided to write a letter to the king himself, an appeal on behalf of your mother."

"But, Sylvie," I exclaimed, clapping my hands, "that is wonderful."

"It would be wonderful if he would tell Monsieur de Lancre that he is doing it. But he is afraid to do so. He fears that Monsieur de Lancre will be so quick in his accusations and his justice that even his wife could become a victim. Therefore he is writing secretly and refuses to interfere until he has the official backing of the court in Paris."

"But Mama could be dead by then," I cried.

"And so could you," Raymond said. "You must do as I suggest."

"Sylvie, Raymond has urged me to go into hiding near here because Pierre has accused me of witchcraft," I said. "But I cannot desert Mama."

"If you can hide somewhere around here and not be discovered," Sylvie said, "then I promise to do my best to sneak you in to see your mama at night. I think I'm clever enough to trick her jailer into vacating his post every once in a while."

"Thank you, Sylvie," I said, giving her a huge hug. "I don't know why you're taking so many risks, but I am grateful."

"I told you why," she muttered, a blush coming to her cheek. "Your mother is worth a hundred Monsieur de Lancres and a thousand fancy doctors."

"Don't *I* get any thanks?" Raymond grinned, waiting for his hug.

That brought a blush to *my* cheek.

"The problem is," he continued, "how to get you out of the village without anyone seeing you."

"I think perhaps I know a way," I answered. "What if I go off to the woods by the river with my fishing pole? No one will pay attention to that. Everyone will assume that I'll be back by the evening meal. But instead of coming back to the village, I will circle around through the forest and climb up to the hut after sunset, by the light of the moon."

"A good idea," Raymond said, nodding. "In the meantime, I will go up there today and leave blankets and food for you."

"Sylvie, when can I try to see Mama again?" I asked, putting my hand on her arm.

"Wait two nights so I can study our jailer and develop a plan," Sylvie said. "Then come on the third night after the first stars come out. I will meet you around the back near the stables. Now I must go. Good luck," she said. "And don't worry. I will tell your mama you are safe, although I dare not tell her where. If she is tortured she will tell them everything she knows."

At that, Sylvie turned and started on her way up the hill.

"Sylvie," I called, just remembering. "I have made some soup for Mama."

"I will see she eats," Sylvie called back, and then she motioned me to get moving.

"I should leave too," Raymond said. "It is not good if people see us talking too much. They will become suspicious and they will start to question me. I will come to visit you at some point," he promised. "You will not be alone."

"Thank you, Raymond," I managed to reply. And yet I remained frozen to the spot as it struck me how alone I *would* be.

"Go quickly," he urged, looking back at me. "They could come for you at any moment."

"I will," I promised, and finally I hurried into the cottage to fetch my fishing pole.

chapter seven

I forced myself to walk slowly out of the village, fishing pole over my shoulder, and into the quiet of the woods. Once at the river I met one of Raymond's brothers, young Laurent, and my cousin Jean, both fishing. I greeted them and told them I was going to try my luck elsewhere. Jean seemed about to object or to try to stop me, but Raymond's brother diverted him, pretending to have a huge fish on his line, and while Jean was turned away I silently scrambled up the bank and away from them both.

I continued on my way, but this time I skirted the actual bank by staying slightly back and among the first stand of trees. That way I avoided a few other neighbors who were fishing by the river that day. I traveled until I was at the edge of the forest, close to the pastures. Then I settled down under a tree to wait for the sun to set and the moon to rise.

I had brought a flask of water with me and some dried meat and bread. I ate these while I waited and then lay down and looked at the sky through the trees. I thought about the mysterious world God had created and how difficult it was to understand it. Beauty surrounded me. The leaves swayed lightly in the wind, the color of the sky changed gradually from blue to the pinks and mauves of the sunset and then to a deep, deep blue just as the first stars came out.

All the ugliness I had witnessed since Papa's death was in such stark contrast to the physical loveliness surrounding me. I tried to comprehend how my own uncle could have betrayed my mama. It was hard to understand someone driven by greed and jealousy. My father's death had really brought out the worst part of his nature, and his wife's death had driven him to hate Mama as the cause of all his troubles.

But if his betrayal was painful, Father Bernard's was even worse. How could our priest, who should have been our leader, with a pure Christian soul, become so mean and full of hate? He had never liked the fact that people had asked for Mama instead of him when they were ill. Thinking back on it now, I believe he had always been jealous of her. Still, he would have put those feelings aside had she chosen to bed him. I suddenly felt so angry with both men that I had to get up and pace up and down, and even the beautiful surroundings could not comfort me.

As soon as it was completely dark, I made my way up the hill toward Raymond's pastures. It took me a long time to reach the hut, as I had to go carefully. The moon was bright, but I didn't want to fall and twist my leg or foot, and I had to be careful not to spook the sheep I passed nor the sheep-dogs. I did go prepared, however, and when one dog came running after me, I threw him some meat. He immediately became my friend.

The night was cold and I took the shawl I had tucked into

my skirt and placed it around my shoulders. I almost missed the hut completely, as it was just a dull shape in the dark. I did find it at last and let myself in. It was a small wooden structure, big enough to shelter a person from the elements. There was a stone grate for a fire, although I could not light one in case someone from the village noticed. It was very dark, but I did find two quilts and I was thankful for those. I left one on the ground for warmth and put the other over me. I was sure I would be up all night, yet I fell into a restless sleep almost immediately. Perhaps sleep was easier at that point than being awake.

Morning came, and with it a small sense of relief that I had not, as yet, been discovered. But as I began to think about everything, I started to worry. After all, if they were really serious about finding me they only had to get some of the best hunters in the village and some dogs and they could easily track me down. Oh, why had I listened to Raymond? Maybe he was in league with Pierre and Father Bernard and had convinced me to run away so everyone could see for themselves how guilty I was. And then it would be easy to follow my trail and capture me...What had I been thinking the day before? What a fool I'd been! I realized that I would have to find somewhere else to hide—but where?

Just as I was ready to run—run anywhere—Raymond poked his head in the door.

"Good morning!" he said cheerfully. "How are you enjoying your castle?"

I leapt up and pushed past him out the door. There was no one with him. All I saw was empty pasture. I felt quite ashamed of myself—soon I would see only the worst in people.

"Raymond," I said urgently, "it is too easy to follow my trail here. This was foolish. I wasn't thinking clearly yesterday."

"But you needn't worry." Raymond smiled. "My brother Laurent told everyone that you went downstream, not up."

"But Jean was with him," I said.

"But Jean didn't actually see which way you went," Raymond replied. "Whereas Laurent says he did! And, just to be on the safe side, I covered your tracks with mine when I came up the mountainside, so no one will suspect. I do think you'll be safe here for a short while, but..."

"But?"

"But perhaps you should begin to think about really getting away. I could probably find you a horse. Is there anywhere you could go?"

"By myself?" I replied, the dismay showing in my face and voice. "I would probably be just as safe here, being tried for a witch, as on the road, a woman alone. Even you would find it dangerous traveling on your own," I added.

Raymond sighed. "I'm afraid there is some truth to what you say."

"I'm not going anywhere yet," I said. "Not until I see Mama. If no one else can help her, I must. I will see her. Perhaps I can help her escape. I have to try."

Raymond nodded. "Of course I understand you wish to help your mama, Rose—but really, what can you do? She is guarded, and even if you do manage to get her out of the chateau, they will quickly notice she is gone and then you will *both* be caught."

"I am going to try," I said firmly.

"I can see you are quite stubborn," Raymond said, but his voice sounded as if that was a quality he rather admired.

"Yes," I agreed, "I am."

"Well, then, it is useless to attempt to dissuade you. I will try to come tomorrow, but I do not want to raise any suspicions. Today I told Papa I would be here checking on the pasture. In fact, he expects me to spend the morning."

"You will be here all morning?" I said.

He nodded. "I hope you don't mind."

"Not at all," I answered. And then quietly added, "I should be glad of the company."

We settled down in the sun, our backs against the hut. Suddenly we both became tongue-tied, and the silence stretched out before us like endless fields of waving wheat. Finally, looking at him from the corner of my eye, I cleared my throat and spoke.

"Raymond," I said, "Sylvie has told me why she is helping me, but...well, why are you helping me as well?"

Raymond looked down at the dirt and paused before he answered. "I suppose you hadn't heard yet."

"Heard what?"

"Before your father died, he and my father had almost concluded the work on a marriage contract for the two of us."

"What!" I exclaimed.

"Your mother had told you nothing?" he asked. And then *his* face flushed. "So then perhaps you do not approve?"

Well, by then I was so embarrassed and tongue-tied, I could barely speak. What could I say to him? "Raymond, it is my dream come true"? Instead I said, "No, she had told me nothing...but, well, perhaps from a few comments I *might* have made, she understood that I would not be against such a match."

"So you wouldn't mind?" he asked.

I looked at the dirt at my feet as I could not look into his eyes.

"I would be happy," I answered. But then the impossibility of the situation rushed over me again and I looked at him and exclaimed, "Oh, what does it matter? It will never happen. It would be better for you to have nothing to do with me—an accused witch."

Raymond spoke softly. "I want to help you, Rose. Please let me do this."

I nodded, for I could not find the words to answer him. My heart was too full. What a wonderful husband he would have made, what a happy life we could have had, and now—now I would be lucky to escape with my life. I was filled with such anger, such a sense of loss, that for a moment I was quite overcome. I believe he understood something of what I was feeling, and perhaps even felt some of those things too, for he turned his head away.

"It's Father Bernard who makes me the angriest," I said, thinking of those who had helped bring this catastrophe down on me and my mama. "He's known us all our lives and yet he is helping this evil judge destroy our village."

"Father Bernard taught me to read and write," Raymond said. "Frankly, I never found him to be good company."

"I wish I could read and write," I said. "I would like to write down all of Mama's cures so other people can use them. I would like to write to my brothers—who knows what my uncle or even Father Bernard wrote to them."

"I'll teach you," Raymond said.

"You will?"

"Yes, and we can start right now," he said. He picked up a stick and looked around for a sandy patch of ground. "Over here, Rose," he called, and then he knelt, smoothing the sand out with his hands.

It was a wonderful idea. It kept my mind off Mama and my troubles, and it gave us something to do, as we were still quite shy with each other. I learned quickly and could write half the alphabet by midday.

Finally, Raymond stood up to leave. We stood awkwardly for a moment. Then he took my hands in his and slowly brought them to his lips for a gentle kiss. I hoped my face wasn't as red as it felt, for he gave me a quick glance, turned and practically ran down the mountain. It was terrible to be alone after that, but I was at least a bit more relaxed in my mind. I wasn't as worried that a mob from the village would suddenly descend on me, and I rested as much as I could, knowing I would need my strength. I forced myself to eat for the same reason.

The next day, although I waited all day for him, Raymond did not appear. This did not surprise me, for I knew that he would not want to make his father or his neighbors suspicious. Still, I was lonely, and with no one to keep me company and no work to occupy me I could not help but worry and fret about Mama. The second night passed even colder than the first and I slept little. In fact, I ended up walking all night, wrapped in my quilts, just to keep warm. When daybreak came and the earth began to warm, I fell asleep in the sun. Again Raymond did not appear.

I began to get nervous as the sun set and the first stars

showed themselves. I walked down from the pastures then, hurrying, worried I had waited too long. It was well into moonrise when I arrived at the chateau. I scurried to the back where the horses were stabled. I was quiet and did not disturb them. And then Sylvie arrived, just as she'd promised.

"Ah, Sylvie, thank heavens," I whispered. "How is Mama?"

"Are *you* all right?" Sylvie asked.

"I'm fine, Sylvie. How is Mama?"

"She is to be examined first thing in the morning," Sylvie replied.

"Where?" I asked.

"They have been granted the use of one of the master's rooms."

"Can I see her, Sylvie?" I asked. "Have you arranged it?"

"Yes," Sylvie replied. "I have quite a simple little plan. You can see her for a short while. The entire village is searching for you," she added. "You mustn't be caught."

"Bless you, Sylvie," I said. "You're an angel."

"Just remember me in your prayers," Sylvie said.

Those words gave me a terrible jolt, for I realized that I had not uttered one prayer to God over the last few days. Quickly I muttered under my breath, "Blessed Virgin, please forgive me and intercede for me with our Lord. I have not forgotten Him. I have just mixed Him up a little with Father Bernard in my head. But He is not Father Bernard, so please watch over Mama and me—and of course Sylvie."

"Not now," Sylvie chided me. "No time for prayers now. Come, follow me."

She took me into the chateau through a side entrance and we hurried into the cellar corridor. She opened a door to a small room and put me inside.

"Your mother and her guard are around the corner, but I have found his weakness. Just give me a short time and I will lead him away. Peek around the corner to make sure all is clear. Your mother's room will be the one with the empty stool outside the door."

She slipped away then and I could hear her calling, "Monsieur Porret, Monsieur Porret, I have a treat for you."

"What is it?"

"It is the kind of treat you can only find in the kitchen. A veal pie, filled with mushrooms and nuts, baked by the chief cook. I pleaded with her to let me have you taste some, but she said only if she herself could watch you eat it—to see the expression on your face as you savored each bite."

He paused for a minute to think about it and I held my breath.

"Well, the witch is asleep anyway, so all right, I'll come."

As I heard their footsteps retreat, I peeked out the door and stepped around the corner. I ran toward the empty stool and gently opened the door to Mama's room. She was not asleep. She was standing, waiting for me. I flew into her arms and wept, and she wept too.

"My little flower," she said. "You are safe?"

"Yes, Mama."

"It is too dangerous for you to come here. I want you to escape. You must go and find your brothers."

"No, Mama, I will *not* leave you as long as there is a chance I can help you. The door is unlocked. Come with me now. We will escape together!"

"No! My jailer will be back in a moment. He will find me gone, he will alert the other guards, and we will *both* be hunted down before we even leave the chateau grounds. I do not think I will escape my tormentors. It is *you* we must think of now."

I could not accept that. "You will escape, Mama. We'll think of a way! I am hiding somewhere they won't think to look. Please come now." And I began to pull her.

"No, child, take yourself away. Only that will give me peace of mind."

"Mama, I could not live with myself knowing I had left you like this. You would not wish me to carry that burden all my life, would you?"

"I care not what burden you carry, Daughter," Mama said fiercely, "as long as you live. You will see that your escape, alone, was the only answer."

"If you will not come with me, Mama, I will not leave the village—not yet. Not until you agree to come."

"Stubborn, stubborn," Mama muttered as she gave me a hug with all her strength.

I kissed her cheeks and thought, And I know where I get that from. Then I turned, ran out the door, closed it and ran back to my little room. Soon after, I heard Sylvie and Mama's jailer return. Mama had been right. We wouldn't even be out of the chateau grounds before her jailer realized she was gone. He would have raised an alarm and we both would have been caught. I had not thought anything out properly, I chided myself. I needed a real plan to get her out of the chateau with all those guards around.

"And where was the cook?" I heard him say.

"She got tired of waiting for you and went to bed, I

suppose," Sylvie retorted. "But was that not a delicious pie?"

"Most satisfactory," the man replied. "Oh, my witch is still fast asleep."

"I must be off," Sylvie said. "The mistress may need me."

I heard her steps go down the hall and then turn in to my corridor. I peeked my head out and she motioned me to follow her. I tiptoed, so he could hear only Sylvie's shoes, and tried to catch up with her. I wanted to tell her I'd decided to stay in my hiding spot. My plan, thought up that minute, was to watch the guard until he, hopefully, fell asleep—that would be my chance to rescue Mama. We would have a head start of at least a few hours while the guard slept. But Sylvie moved swiftly ahead of me, obviously anxious to get me safely out of the chateau. I dared not call ahead to her for fear Mama's guard would hear. Once we were on the main floor I called out, as quietly as I could.

"Sylvie, wait!"

She stopped and turned toward me.

"What is it?" she whispered as I hurried up to her.

"I've decided to stay downstairs, watch the guard and try to free Mama."

"You put yourself in great danger," Sylvie warned. "Your mama would not approve."

"I do not care if she approves or not!" I argued. "I will drag her out if I need to. Please, I must go back."

Just then, much to our horror, we heard the sound of voices coming our way.

"Quickly, in there!" Sylvie ordered, and she opened the door nearest us, pushing me ahead of her. We waited in the light of Sylvie's candle. My heart pounded and I could barely breathe. The voices came closer and closer. Sylvie looked around.

"There," she said, pointing to a series of screens along the wall. "Hide. In case they come in here."

"What about you?" I said, grabbing her sleeve.

"Best for me to be out in the open, not caught hiding. That would look too suspicious. Go!"

I scampered over to the screens and crouched behind them. Seconds later I heard the doors being flung open. I could not see who it was, of course, but there were two male voices.

"And what are you doing here?" one exclaimed to Sylvie.

"I live in this house, monsieur," Sylvie retorted, "and do not need to explain my presence or my mistress's wishes to *you*! What are you doing here?"

"I am to make this room ready for the questioning at break of day," the man answered.

"*This* room?" Sylvie repeated.

"That is correct. This room is the one your master has allowed us. This and no other, he said. So I will make it ready." He paused. "With your permission," he added sarcastically.

"Of course," Sylvie murmured, and then louder, "I will leave you now." The last was for my benefit, no doubt.

I was trapped! Now, not only could I not try my plan of rescue, but I was in serious danger of being discovered by M. de Lancre's men. Still, I hoped they would have no reason to move the screens, and I also hoped that their preparations would be quick, still giving me time to help Mama.

Both hopes, however, proved fruitless. Saying little, the men went about their jobs, speaking only to convey instructions to one another. I was so nervous that I barely heard what they said, always waiting for them to move the screens and discover me. I felt that surely once their job was done they would leave for their rest, but it seemed to take them hours. And then I heard a chair scrape, and one said to the other that he would go get some rest.

At that point I dared to peek out a crack between two screens and saw, to my dismay, a man sitting at a desk, copying. How long would he be there? I slumped to the floor and tried to hold back my tears. And I prayed for him to go. Every minute seemed to last forever; no night had ever lasted so long.

Finally, I heard the cock crow and I could not stop the tears. My hopes were in ruins. Mama would be questioned and I could not stop it. Then a terrible realization struck me. I would be forced to watch them question, perhaps torture, my mama.

chapter eight

By kneeling just in front of the crack between the two screens I had a good view of the center of the room. It was an inner room, with no natural light from windows—no doubt chosen by the master just for that reason, so servants could not glimpse what was happening. Candles on the desk gave off the only light. Soon servants entered with lamps, and shortly after that the great doors of the room swung open and Father Bernard marched in, followed by M. de Lancre and one of his men. Each man carried a number of different items. Father Bernard had with him paper and his quills and ink. The two other men had strangely constructed instruments and ropes. Could I sit here and watch them torture Mama?

The men busied themselves with what I assumed were final preparations. One of them was a large man with thick gray hair and hanging jowls; the other, the fellow who had been copying, was a slim fellow with a gray complexion who looked as if he'd never smiled a day in his life.

Father Bernard addressed M. de Lancre as the men tested a rope with a pulley attached to it that had been thrown over a beam in the ceiling.

"Monsieur," he said, "I should like to come to some agreement in respect to Madame Suzanne Rives's property."

"Her estate," Monsieur de Lancre replied, "will, of course, pay for all the expenses incurred by this trial and by her imprisonment. We must pay the count, after all, for his hospitality. Monsieur Belot, the torturer, must be paid, as well as Monsieur Clerve, the recorder; Monsieur Porret, the guard; and you too, Father, for you will be writing down all this for the Church's records. Ordinarily anything left would go to her daughter. But now that her daughter has also been declared a witch, all their property will be forfeit. I suggest that the Church receive twenty percent of whatever is left, and the parliament of Montpellier, as represented by myself, receive the other eighty percent."

"With all due respect," Father Bernard objected, "I believe all her estates should revert to the Church. I can then sell them back to her dead husband's family for a tidy sum. After all," he remarked, "it was my testimony that first made you aware of her."

"Yours *and* the good doctor's," M. de Lancre corrected. "But all right, we'll say thirty for you, seventy for us."

"Forty for us, sixty for you," Father Bernard suggested, "if you agree to sell the lands back to the family."

"Agreed," M. de Lancre grumbled. "We are really not interested in the land itself—only the wealth that can be derived from it. When we had our hunt in Montpellier, it enriched everyone in the town: the scribes, the torturers, the prison guards, the lawyers, the judges, the clergy, the craftsmen who built the stakes, the innkeeper who had extra trade because of the crowds...Oh, yes, these burnings were a great thing for the city. It is wonderful to see that not only can we cleanse an entire city, an entire region, of the devil, but others and ourselves can also profit from all this."

"It is the Lord's way," Father Bernard said.

The Lord's way. I couldn't believe my own ears. Surely this was some terrible nightmare from which I would awaken. The Church, God's representatives here on earth, bartering over Mama's property, gloating over all the money they would get from her suffering. And this judge, the representative of the law, direct from the parliament of Montpellier, gleefully crowing over the profit he was making from these women's agony. I wanted to rush out and confront both those men right then, but what good would that have done? I forced myself to control my rage.

The doors opened and M. Porret came in pulling someone behind him. To my surprise, it was not Mama who was brought in but Mme Trembley. And suddenly I remembered her warning on the day that Papa died, the day Mama saved the baby and became a target for both Father Bernard and the doctor. She'd screamed of a fire consuming us all; she'd *seen* the future. Did that make her a witch? But some people had the talent of seeing and used it to help—why did that have to be the devil's work?

The poor woman was forced to stand in the middle of the room, and then two servant girls were brought in and told to strip off her clothes. Left only in her shift, she was then walked over to the rope. I could see that she had already been tortured. Her fingers seemed crushed, her shift was covered in dried blood, she had burn marks on her wrists and ankles. She looked around in terror and whimpered pitifully.

"Please, Your Honors, do not hurt me again. Just tell me what to say and I will say it. It's just that I don't know what you want me to say."

"Tell us about your broomstick," the judge commanded. "How did you make it fly?"

"I—I don't know," she replied.

"Bind her," the judge ordered.

"No, no!" she screamed, but she was bound very tight by the big man with the jowls.

The torturer approached her with a small clamp, which he attached to her thumb. He began to tighten a screw in this clamp until Mme Trembley screamed and cried.

"How did you make your broomstick fly?" M. de Lancre repeated. "Did you use ointment?"

"Yes, yes, I used ointment for it," she panted. "I rubbed it with ointment."

"And where did you fly?"

"To meet with other witches."

"Aha! There were others? Who were they?"

"But I don't know," she cried. "What others?"

"The other witches you met. Who were they?"

"I can't think."

Then M. de Lancre motioned to the torturer, who left the thumbscrew on but attached the poor woman to the pulley by the cords that bound her hands behind her back. Slowly he pulled on the rope until she was lifted and dangled in the air, her arms stretched out above her. She cried and moaned.

"I will tell you anything, only let me down."

"No, you will not be let down until you *do* tell us everything," M. de Lancre said. And then he motioned to the torturer, who suddenly let go of the rope so that Mme Trembley dropped toward the ground and was pulled up short. She let out a terrible scream, for her shoulders must have been nearly pulled out of their sockets.

"If you do not tell us all the names," M. de Lancre's voice boomed, "we will put stones on your legs and draw you up and then let you drop again."

"But I cannot think!" she cried.

"Picture the streets of your village," M. de Lancre instructed. "Go up and down them in your mind and picture who lives in each house. Then try to remember if that person was at your sabbat, your meeting with the devil. And what did you do at these meetings?"

"I don't know."

"Did you dance, and pledge your loyalty to him?"

"Yes, we danced and pledged our loyalty to him," Mme Trembley whimpered.

"And *who* was there?"

"I think it was Madame Baille...Yes, she was there, and Madame Aurilhac and Madame De Cervello and Madame Gaillac."

Oh, no, I thought, that is Raymond's mother.

"And Madame Rives, was she there too?"

"Yes, yes, she was there too."

"And her daughter?"

"Yes, her daughter too."

"And any more?"

"I can't remember any more. It hurts. It hurts too much."

And then M. de Lancre motioned for the torturer to lower Mme Trembley, and she sprawled moaning on the floor.

"Who is your familiar?" M. de Lancre continued, but the old woman was unconscious and could not answer.

"Take her back to the cellar," the judge ordered, "and get the doctor to look after her. Tell him we don't want her to die, as we have to question her further, so make sure she is kept warm and given some broth. Also, she must be well enough to sign her confession so we can read it out at her burning." The torturer and the two servant girls carried her out of the room.

"Well." M. de Lancre smiled. "That was productive. She has named four other women. What is their standing in the community?" he asked Father Bernard.

"Only Madame De Cervello is a widow," Father Bernard stated, "so we could expect *all* her property. Still, Madame Gaillac is from the wealthiest family in the village, and they will pay well for her trial." He shook his head. "I would not have thought that Madame Gaillac would be a witch. She always seemed a good woman to me."

"Ah, yes, Father, but that is the way they fool us. They use their powers to make us believe they are good Christian women, while all the time they are meeting secretly with the devil, having lewd sexual relations with him, poisoning children, raising tempests...Look into the eyes of a witch and there you will see pure evil. And like Eve, Father, they tempt us always into unclean thoughts."

"How true that is!" Father Bernard exclaimed. "That is what Suzanne Rives did to me, a holy Father of the Catholic Church. She bewitched me until all I could do was think lustful thoughts about her. It was a terrible torture for my soul."

"You will be freed when her body burns, Father, and she has confessed and finally goes to our Lord."

"Yes," Father Bernard said fiercely, "then and only then will I be free."

"And what of her daughter?" M. de Lancre asked. "Any word on her yet?"

"I have sent two men after her, one on the northern road and one on the southwestern. I am sure one of them will track her down."

At least I will not give them *that* satisfaction, I thought. And I prayed I would not give them the satisfaction of discovering me here, either.

"Well, then, Father, let us bring the mother in for her first appearance before us." M. de Lancre waved at the recorder to go and get her.

M. de Lancre continued to talk to Father Bernard, his voice cheerful. "We were fortunate that Madame Trembley is so weak. We did not have to bother with the final or extraordinary torture in order to get names from her—she confessed with just the use of ordinary torture. She may recant, of course, once she is feeling better, but I think we need only have tied her up to the strappado once again for her to agree that all she said was the truth after all. She is but a simple woman, however. This other one may need all the levels of torture before she will name her accomplices—and of course she *must* name her daughter, as we already know she is a witch. I would like to conclude all of this quickly, for I cannot stay too long in such a small village when I have many larger towns yet to visit."

Father Bernard readied a fresh quill and fresh paper. And then they brought in Mama. My heart broke to look at her. I was in a terrible state of shock after what I had just seen and heard, and now I was truly terrified as to what they would do to her. I saw that they were not looking for proof of any kind—they did not even have witnesses present to accuse the women of specific crimes. The women were guilty once accused, and the rest was simply a matter of making them admit it. Mama had been right. There was no hope for her to escape death. Only if the king himself intervened in time would she, possibly, be allowed to live. But from what M. de Lancre had just said, he would not stay here long and would probably put Mama to extreme torture to get her to confess quickly.

I had to get Mama out. I needed another plan. They sat Mama down in a chair and began to question her.

chapter nine

M. de Lancre picked up a book from the table and began to read questions from it.

"Madame Rives, how long have you been a witch?"

"I am no witch," Mama answered.

"Why did you become a witch?"

"I did not," she said. "I deny it."

"How did you become a witch and what happened on that occasion?"

"I did not, sir!"

"What was the name of your master among the evil demons?"

"I have only the Lord as my Master," my mother replied. "And I pray to Him to help me in my hour of need."

"That is enough!" M. de Lancre's voice boomed. "I will not hear the Lord's name taken in vain in such a way. You will tell us all, Madame, never fear. Strip her," he ordered.

Mama was pulled up from her chair and stripped of her clothes by the two servants. This time at least she was allowed to keep her shift on, and then her hands and feet were bound tight with a cord.

"This is what you will endure, Madame, if you do not speak." M. de Lancre then showed her the instruments of torture. "Thumbscrews will crush your nails at the roots. You will be dropped on the strappado, or perhaps we'll use these for your eyes" he held up a small hook just large enough to tear the eye out "or—"

"Stop!" Mama screamed at him. "You are an evil man. I will not listen to you. I have done no wrong. If you are going to torture me, get on with it. I will admit everything and then take it all back when you are finished. What is the point of that?"

"There will be a time, Madame, when you will no longer take it back," M. de Lancre said. "Just looking at our instruments will remind you of the unbearable pain and you will not want to go through it again, so you will admit that everything you confessed under torture was true. That is the only way to make a witch tell the truth."

"Father, you have known me many years," Mama pleaded, looking at him. "Why have you turned on me this way?"

"You are a true daughter of Eve," Father Bernard said. "There is not a more important story in the Bible than that of Adam and Eve. From the beginning, woman has been evil, a temptress, and man a poor victim of her wiles. We protect ourselves as well as we can, yet still you bewitch us..."

"I did not bewitch you, Father. I never wanted your advances. You punish me now because of that. Had I agreed, you would be protecting me now instead of standing in judgment of me."

"Nothing you say is the truth," Father Bernard seethed. "Only under torture will the truth be known. The Holy Inquisition has tried many like you over generations, and we know how evil you are, what lies you tell. Now this good judge has taken up the work of the Inquisition and I will help him, for it is holy work."

And then they attached a vise to Mama's thumbs and screwed it tighter and tighter until she screamed, and I had to hold my hand over my mouth to stop from screaming too. I had once caught my thumb in a doorjamb, and I remember the pain as almost unbearable. This would be like that a thousandfold.

M. de Lancre began his questions again.

"How long have you been a witch?"

"I am not!" she cried.

"Why did you become a witch?"

"I did not!"

"How did you become a witch?"

"I have not!"

M. de Lancre motioned for them to sit her down. The torturer left the room. When he came back he had a kettle of boiling water. He pulled a wide boot onto her leg and held the kettle over it. Mama groaned.

"Please, no," she pleaded.

And then he poured the water down the boot.

Her screams were too terrible to bear. I had to bite my hand until it bled so as not to give myself away.

Finally they took the boot off and the water ran over the floor. M. de Lancre said, "How long have you been a witch?"

"For years now," Mama sobbed.

"How many years?"

"I don't know."

"How many?"

"For ten years."

"Why did you become a witch?"

"Because—because the devil convinced me to."

"How did you become a witch and what happened on that occasion?"

"The devil told me I must attend a meeting," Mama panted, "and so I went."

"Do you mean a sabbat?"

"Yes, a sabbat."

"How did you go?"

"I don't know."

"Did you fly?"

"Yes, I flew."

"On your broomstick?"

"Yes."

"How did you make it fly? With spells or ointments?"

"With special ointments the devil gave me."

"And what happened once you were there?"

Mama was crying so hard she could barely answer. Her leg was red, the color of a poppy.

"I don't know."

"Did you dance with the devil?"

"Yes, I danced with him."

"And there was a banquet?"

"Yes."

"And what food was served?"

"What food?"

"Yes, what food?"

"Ah, venison, and rabbit."

"And did you have intercourse with the devil?"

"Yes."

"And what injuries have you done to your neighbors?"

"Injuries?" And then Mama seemed to remember herself and said, "But I never injured. I have only cured."

"The devil makes you say that!" M. de Lancre thundered. And he walked up to her and kicked her on her burned leg.

She screamed and cried, "Yes, I have poisoned little children. Little Pierre, who died two years ago, he died because I gave him poison, and then I made it seem as if he had died of fever."

"And your sister-in-law? Did you not poison her as well?"

"Yes, yes, of course."

"And Madame the Countess's baby? Were you not planning to sacrifice her to your lord?"

And then Mama looked at him with a look of such pain, to be forced to say such things. Her eyes closed and she fell from her chair unconscious.

Tears streamed down my face and I prayed to the Lord to take my life away, for the earth was too cruel a place in which to live and I could bear no more.

But as they carried Mama out I realized that it was *she* who was suffering, not me, and that I could not give in to my grief. I had to save her. Somehow.

When she was gone, M. de Lancre rubbed his hands together.

"That was a good day's work," he said, "and it has made me very hungry. You two clean up in here," he said to the servant girls. "We will all go for the midday meal. Then we must think about arresting these other women. A few more of my men arrived last night, by the way," he said to Father Bernard on the way out. "I thought we might need them in case some of the husbands or sons become angry. If that happens, I think all these women should be brought to the jails in Montpellier. Easier to protect them there from relatives who might mistakenly wish to free them."

And on that note, they left the room. The servant girls brought in pails of water and scrubbed the floors down. They talked to each other as they worked.

"Who would have thought," said one, "that Madame Rives was a witch. And all the nasty things she has done to people, killing her own sister-in-law!"

The other shook her head. "I never liked Madame Trembley. She cursed me many a time when I wouldn't feed her scraps from the kitchen. And one time after she cursed me I took sick and was in bed for a week!"

And so they chattered and worked until finally everything was clean and they departed. It was a long wait until nightfall, I realized, until Sylvie could come and get me, so I tried to get comfortable and not think about what I had just seen.

But Sylvie surprised me. She entered the room shortly after the servants left, running over to where I hid behind the screens.

"Everyone is at the midday meal," she whispered. "Come on." And she hurried me down the stairway to the cellar. Even the jailer was gone.

Once we were safely in the cellar corridor, Sylvie stopped to talk to me.

"I'm sorry I had to leave you there," she said. "I watched the room all night, but there was never a time I could safely get you out."

"I know that," I said. "How is Mama?"

Sylvie shook her head. "It must have been terrible, what they did to her. She is quite poorly. The only reason you can visit her is that her guard is no longer worried about watching her. She cannot walk. Come."

I tried to harden myself before I entered Mama's room. I had to be strong for her. She did not need my tears now.

She was stretched out on the camp bed on a blanket, her leg covered in salve. It was red, and she moaned quietly.

"Mama," I whispered as I bent over her.

She looked at me and clutched my hand. "Rose, my little flower."

I had wanted to be strong, but, looking at her, all I could do was blame myself. I broke down and began to cry.

"I was there, Mama. I saw everything."

"You were there?" Mama cried.

"We were caught unexpectedly," Sylvie explained. "I had to hide Rose behind the screens to prevent them finding her. She was there throughout."

Before Mama could say anything, I exploded.

"They are monsters. How can a person call himself human and do such a thing? Oh, Mama," I cried, "it is all my fault. If only I'd helped you escape—now you can't walk and all is lost." I slumped beside her, my head on the bed, and sobbed.

"Rose," Mama said, "listen to me. Do not blame yourself. I will not have it. None of this is your fault. It is those men, and blame begins and stops with them. There was no way to get me out of here once I was held and guarded. We would have needed at least a four- or five-hour head start, but we would have had only minutes." She paused. "Still, there is something you can do for me, but it is a huge thing to ask."

"What, Mama? Anything."

"Go to our cottage and find the poppy mixture I use to calm patients and to ease their pain. Bring it here to me."

"But why?"

"Because, child, if they put me to the torture again, I will tell them anything. I will name my neighbors and doom them to this same fate. I cannot do that and go clean to God. Please, Rose, do this for me. And then you must escape. Promise me."

"But there must be a way to help you, Mama. The count has written the king. If you could just hold out a little longer."

"Perhaps the king will intervene for others, Rose, but for me it will be too late. Please, Rose, I do not wish to suffer anymore."

"But, Mama, to kill yourself is a mortal sin."

She looked at me then and did not speak. I knew that I had to do it.

"Mama," I whispered and clutched her hands. "Please do not leave me here alone. Let me go too. Let me drink the potion with you. Then we can both be with Papa. Mama, please, it is too hard to stay here in this life after what I have seen."

Mama held my hands tight and looked me in the eye. Despite her pain, a little strength seemed to return to her eyes.

"Rose, I will not drink the potion unless you promise me that you will live. And if I do not drink, you will have to see me suffer even more."

"But, Mama, that isn't fair."

"I don't care if it is fair or not fair. You are going to live. I know that Raymond loves you. You can still have a life. Your brothers will find you. They'll take care of you. And, Rose, there are many lives that *you* can save, many people for you to take care of, people who will need your gift of healing."

"*My* gift?"

"Yes, little flower. You know you are as gifted a healer as I am. Gifts from God must not be wasted."

At that I let out a long sigh and nodded my head. "All right, Mama. I will live—if they let me."

"Promise me, Rose."

"I promise. I will bring the potion tonight." And then I bent over and kissed her gently on her forehead.

Sylvie pulled me out of the room and down the corridor to a tiny room. "In here," she said. "I'll come back for you tonight to help you get out of the chateau."

I nodded and sank to my knees, forgetting even to thank her. Somehow I had to figure out how to get home, get the potion and return safely. I also had to figure out how I could find the strength to help kill my own mother.

chapter ten

Well into the first hour of sleep, Sylvie came to fetch me.

"I will watch for you by the kitchen door," she whispered as we hurried through the chateau corridors. "That way, if anyone discovers me I can claim I came down for a small meal."

"Sylvie," I whispered, "if it were you, if it were your mother, would you do as she asked?"

"Yes," Sylvie said without any hesitation, "I would, most certainly. My uncle told me that some women accused of being witches in his town tried to kill themselves but were prevented from doing so. They were forced to suffer—some for months, some for years—while their trials went forward. I would not wish that on your mother."

"They won't make Mama suffer for that long," I replied. "They are determined to extract a confession quickly. But she is in terrible agony." And then I said, "It's not fair! Mama has been good and honest and tried to help people all her life. It seems her only crime is that she is a woman—as Father Bernard says, a daughter of Eve!"

"That's crime enough for most of them." Sylvie snorted.

By this time we had reached the kitchen door. I squeezed Sylvie's hand and crept out into the night.

As I hurried down the chateau road to the village, I neared Raymond's house and realized I had to warn him about his mother. She had to escape and she had to do it that night. When I got to their house I slipped through the gate and into their yard. I knocked at the door. The dogs began to bark. Be quiet, I prayed, or the entire village will know I'm here.

Mercifully, M. Gaillac soon came to the door. He looked at me questioningly. He had obviously been sound asleep. Seconds later Raymond was standing behind him, fully dressed, looking wide awake.

"Papa, let Rose in, hurry," Raymond said.

M. Gaillac opened the door and I slipped in. Mme Gaillac was coming down the stairs; she, too, looked sleepy. I was relieved to see her. At least they had not come for her yet.

"Ah, Madame, you are here!" I exclaimed. "Thank God."

"And where should I be?" she asked.

"Madame, I'm afraid you are in terrible danger," I said. "I was in the room when they questioned Madame Trembley. They tortured her. They made her name other women as witches. It wasn't her fault—she named you, Madame. You are accused of being a witch." Mme Gaillac gasped and put her hand to her throat.

Raymond looked at his mother, then at me.

"Come sit," Raymond urged me. "You look dreadful, Rose." He made me sit at the kitchen table and gave me a glass of ale. He brought mugs for his father and mother too, and when he gave his mother the drink, he gave her a kiss as well.

"Mama," he said, "you must run away, and it must be tonight. They will certainly come for you in the morning."

"No, this cannot be true." His mother began to cry. "Will they force me to leave my husband, my family, run away from my entire life? Then I don't want to live!"

M. Gaillac held her hand.

"Catherine," M. Gaillac said, and his voice cracked with emotion, "the important thing is for you to survive. This will pass over, somehow we will get your name cleared with the parliament, but Raymond is right. If you stay you will be tortured and you will confess and all will be lost. Besides," he added, "Rose must flee too. They are searching for her everywhere. She needs someone to look after her. You would not let her go alone."

She looked at me and pulled me to her. "Rose, will you go with me?"

I'm sure M. Gaillac knew that using me as a means to make her go would work.

"Yes, Madame, of course," I cried. "You don't know what it would mean to me not to be on my own!"

"I will take you both up to the shed tonight," Raymond declared, "and at first light you can begin your journey. Mama, go and get packed."

Then I thought of my own mother, who would never escape.

"I must do something first, Raymond," I said. "I will have to meet you at the hut."

"No, Rose," he insisted. "You must come now. Anything else is too dangerous. We can bring two donkeys, and you can travel across the mountains into Spain."

"Yes, yes, quite right," M. Gaillac agreed. "The roads to Paris or Montpellier will be watched. They will track you on both of them. The mountains are the only chance. And I agree with Raymond. Rose, you must go now. Every minute you stay here you are in terrible danger. And," he said, patting my hand, "we must keep our future daughter-in-law safe." Then he looked at me. "Did you say you *saw* the trial? Were you *in* the chateau?"

I told them quickly what had happened—everything except Mama's last request. All I said was that she had asked me to do something and I could not refuse. I had to go back to my cottage and then to the chateau.

M. Gaillac began to argue with me and so did Raymond, but Mme Gaillac looked at me and said, "The child has been asked a final favor by her mama. Would you deny her the doing of it?"

That silenced them both. I stood to leave, saying I had to hurry. Mme Gaillac kissed me on the forehead. "Bless you, child. Perhaps you saved my life. I will wait for you at the hut."

I slipped out the door with Raymond behind me.

"You can tell me, Rose," he said.

I couldn't speak and he put his arms around me and held me tight.

"She is in such pain," I whispered. "And she fears naming others—other innocents like your mother." I began to weep. "She just wants to sleep, Raymond. In the arms of God."

Raymond let out a deep sigh. And he whispered back, "You are very brave. My thoughts will be with you."

"Thank you," I said, not sure what I was thanking him for—perhaps for not condemning me, for understanding.

"Hurry," he urged.

"I will," I promised, and I drew away from him, turned and ran to let myself out the gate.

Fortunately I knew the path down past the houses so well I could have done it with a blindfold—and I may as well have, for it was very dark that night. The moon and the stars were covered by clouds, and by the time I reached our cottage, a light rain had begun to fall. I crept inside. It was pitch-dark, and since there was no fire I could not light a candle. Still, I knew where everything was. I inched my way over to the cupboard and felt around for the small jar I knew Mama kept the poppy potion in. I found it and put it in my pocket.

"So you've come back for your evil potions!" A voice crackled in the darkness. I almost leapt out of my skin. I could tell from the voice that it was Pierre. I whirled around to see a dark shape in the doorway.

"You'll have to come with me, witch," he said, his voice triumphant.

It was hard to think quickly, but I turned back to the cupboard and felt for the powders. My hands skimmed lightly over the jars until I found the small round saucer I needed.

"What are you doing?" Pierre demanded. "Get out here or I'll come in there after you."

"Pierre," I said, "you're so brave, hunting down dangerous witches, I don't suppose it will scare you to come in here after me."

And with that I moved quickly to the hearth and placed my free hand on the handle of a pot. Pierre came crashing into the cottage, stubbed his toe on something, cursed and then bumped into the table. As he rounded the table, using both hands to feel where he was going, I could see his shape and knew where I had to aim. I took a couple of steps toward him and threw the pepper into his eyes. He screamed and began to curse and rub his eyes. Before he could get his bearings, I raised up on my toes and brought the pot crashing down on his head. He slumped to the ground without a sound.

Swiftly I moved around his body and raced out the cottage door. I forgot all about sneaking through the village—instead I simply ran at full speed up, up, up the road, and I did not stop until I reached the chateau. By the time I tapped on the kitchen door, I was bathed in sweat and barely able to breathe. Sylvie opened the door for me. She had a small candle in her hand, and she surveyed me with some distress.

"What happened? You look as though you've been to the wars," she whispered.

"I have," I answered. "Pierre. He must have been watching the cottage in case I returned. He tried to capture me."

"Where is he?" she asked, obviously worried.

"He's lying on our cottage floor, a pot implanted in his head!" I replied.

"No more than he deserves. Come on."

I followed her down the now familiar route to Mama's room. Again no guard was there.

"Her jailer was happy to be able to sleep in a bed tonight," Sylvie said. "Your mama is going nowhere."

"How is she?" I asked.

"Not well," Sylvie responded gently. "I think she has a fever coming on. Perhaps the leg is becoming infected. She is in terrible distress and cannot rest—only sometimes she slips into unconsciousness from the pain, and that is a mercy."

The sweat on my body began to turn cold, and I found I was shivering—partly, I am sure, from fear at what I was about to do.

Sylvie was carrying a glass of wine in her hand. When we reached Mama's room, Sylvie held the glass up for me and I took the jar from my pocket.

"A few drops will put someone to sleep," I said. "A large spoonful and they will never wake up."

I spilled at least two spoonfuls into the glass and then handed the jar to Sylvie as she passed me the wineglass.

"I must go back to my room," Sylvie said. "Keep the candle. I can find my way. I have been gone a long time, and sometimes the baby wakes and the mistress calls for me. I dare not stay away longer."

"I will find my way out," I said. "Don't worry. And thank you, Sylvie, thank you. I don't know how to say it well enough."

We kissed each other good-bye, and Sylvie ran down the corridor. Gently I let myself into Mama's room. She was sitting up, her back against the stone wall, her face pale, her leg exposed. The flesh over her leg had tightened and turned a deep reddish purple. I gasped when I saw it.

This time I was determined not to break down as I had done before. I perched on the edge of the cot.

She was very weak. "Rose, my sweet. I know how hard this is for you. It is easier for me. I am going to God and I will see my dear Philippe again. You must stay here and struggle and remember all this horror, But promise me, Rose, that when you think of me it will not be with regret that you couldn't save me—because you *are* doing the one thing you are able to. You are saving my soul." She paused, out of breath. She was very weak. "Rose," she whispered. "Where is my drink, child?"

Reluctantly I held it out to her.

"Talk to me while I drink. Tell me how you will escape."

And so I did. Voice trembling as I helped her drink down the wine, I told her of my meeting with Raymond and his family, how they would help me, how Sylvie had helped me and what our plan was. When I was finished and the glass was empty, she smiled at me.

"You have made me very happy," she murmured. "I knew Raymond was the right boy for you—and see now how well he has proved himself. And his mama will be your mama now, and she will take care of you."

At that I put my cheek beside hers, and my tears slid silently down and mingled with hers.

"Kiss me, Rose," Mama said.

I kissed her gently on the lips and she said, "God bless you and keep you safe." Then she closed her eyes.

"I love you, Mama," I said. I think she heard me, for she smiled a little and then her head sank to her chest. Her breathing was shallow and irregular, and I could tell that very soon she would be dead.

Suddenly, I heard a noise. I don't know what I actually

heard at first, but I knew it wasn't right. And then I could tell it was people shouting and running. I blew out the candle and leapt to my feet. Quickly I ran behind the door just as it flew open, almost crashing into me. Light flared into the room.

"Is she there?" a voice called. It was Pierre.

"No."

"Well, she is somewhere around."

They shut the door, not even noticing that Mama did not wake up with all the clamor. I knew I had to wait until they had searched everywhere in the chateau and left to search the village before I dared to venture out. So I sat beside my mother, held her hand in the dark and wondered how I could join her. I didn't weep. I was too afraid. I just sat and shivered and held Mama's hand and prayed to the Blessed Virgin to help me.

chapter eleven

I couldn't think straight. I couldn't think at all. They were sure to capture me. Images flooded my mind of the torturer and his instruments. Would they gouge out my eyes? Would they string me up like Mme Trembley? Would they scald me as they did Mama? And when they burned me, would they kill me first or burn me alive? Should I confess everything before they tortured me? Even if I did, M. de Lancre would torture me, thinking that I was confessing only to avoid the pain. And he would be right. I trembled and shook from head to foot and prayed alternately for my death or for my release. I cursed myself for leaving the potion with Sylvie. If I'd had it I would most certainly have drunk from it to avoid the agony of torture.

But suddenly the door opened and Sylvie stood there, holding a candle.

"Well," she whispered, "are you just going to sit there or would you like to leave?"

"What?" I replied, stunned.

"I heard they were looking for you," she said, "so I went to Pierre and told him you were probably hiding in Mme Trembley's hut. I hope she will forgive me, but I do not think she can be in any more trouble than she already is. I said I'd seen you hiding there once before during a hide-and-seek game and that you would probably think it a safe place. They've all run off after you, so come, hurry now."

I threw Mama one last look, and then I followed Sylvie.

"You are an angel, Sylvie," I whispered as we got to the kitchen.

Sylvie stopped for a moment before opening the kitchen door.

"It was not really my aunt who was taken by the Inquisition," she said, tears in her eyes. "It was my mama. I have never told anyone—people might think I take after my mother. I didn't feel I could even tell you—under torture you would reveal anything. But you will go to freedom now, and I want you to see me as your sister, in all things." She paused. "Anything I can do to thwart them I will, even at risk to myself."

"I'm so sorry, Sylvie," I said.

"They will not get *us*, though," Sylvie said fiercely. "So off you go now." She gave me a quick hug. I hugged her back and then quickly slipped through the door and out onto the grounds. It was very dark, but the clouds parted every once in a while so I could at least get my bearings. It was not easy climbing the pastures on such a black night. But I persevered, and finally, as the sky began to lighten, I found the hut.

Raymond was waiting for me.

"What happened to you?" he exclaimed. "We have been waiting almost all night."

"Your mother is here too?"

"She is inside."

"I was almost captured," I explained.

"Captured? How? And how did you escape?"

Quickly I told him what had transpired until I escaped. When I was done he took my hand.

"I am so sorry about your mother," he said.

"So am I," I said. "I hope those men go straight to hell."

"I must leave now," Raymond said, "and go over your tracks with my own. I covered Mama's and mine with a branch as we walked. I shall have to do the same for yours. Mama gave me some herbs and spices to throw on the ground near the chateau where you began your climb, so the dogs will be fooled by the smells and lose your scent. Still, if I don't run now it will be too late."

I nodded my agreement.

"Mama suggests that you can pose as a mother and daughter who make their living by working the land for others. You can tell people that you travel from place to place seeking work."

I felt that this was a good plan. People like that were common everywhere, and no one would question us.

"Rose," Raymond said, "may I kiss you farewell?"

I nodded and raised my head, for even though I was very tall, he was a head taller yet. He kissed me, and I must say it was wonderful, soft and tender—only afterward I once again felt that terrible sense of loss, the sense of what might have been. Then he opened the door to the hut.

"Mama, Rose is here."

"I know," I heard her reply. "But I thought you two might want some words alone."

His mother came out of the hut. She looked very sad and old. Her eyes were red and there were deep circles under them. She opened her arms to me and I ran into them. She held me tight.

"It is a terrible thing, child, what has happened. Your poor mother is a good, no, a great woman. And here we two are forced to leave everything we know and love...But this is no time for crying. We must be on our way or we will be captured as well."

She let go of me and clasped Raymond to her.

"I love you, my dear," she said. "I pray to the Holy Virgin that I will see you again."

"You will, Mama. I promise. I will come for you when this is all over. I will come for both of you."

"But we will never be able to return," I said. "We are witches now."

"Then I will come live where you are!" Raymond declared.

And with that he turned, picked up a long branch with the leaves still on it and began to sweep and run down the hill the way I had come up.

The cock would crow soon. Behind the shed two mules were tethered, one laden with supplies, one saddled.

"We can take turns riding," Raymond's mother said.

"You ride first, Madame," I insisted.

"You may not call me Madame," she said, looking very stern.

"What shall I call you?"

"You will call me Mama, as I *am* to be your future mother-in-law."

I was so thankful to be with her, and yet when she said that, although I was grateful, I could not help but see *my* mama, alone in a cold room, her body to be put to the fire. I wondered if a heart could really break from pain and if mine would do just that.

"Yes, Mama," I murmured, and I took my mule's reins as she mounted.

"Raymond said that we should follow this path until it reaches the small road that twists through the mountains," she said. "And my two other sons have taken horses and are riding on the Paris road—when their tracks are discovered, everyone will think it is us, so we have quite a good start. That was Raymond's idea," she said proudly. "He is very clever."

And so we began. As the day wore on I tried to fix everything that had happened in my memory. I felt that if we survived the journey and the years of exile, and if Raymond found me and married me, perhaps he would write it down for me. Or better yet, perhaps he would finish teaching *me* to write and I would write it all down myself. So others could be warned.

It seemed to me, as I walked, that I could hear the screams of women as they were humiliated and then tortured. I could hear their agony as they were burned alive at the stake. Perhaps there were real witches somewhere. But all the ones I had seen accused were women, that's all—simple women with none but the ordinary flaws of character we are all subject to. I hoped never to hear the word *witch* again, but I knew it would visit me in my dreams and I would see the boiling water and the hot flames and I would weep.

postscript

I am adding this postscript, having written down this story to the best of my ability. Five years have passed since M. de Lancre first came to our village. With the count's help, the court in Paris reviewed Mama's case and those of the other women in our village. It was decided that all the trials, except Mme Trembley's, were carried out in excessive haste and that the women were of pure character after all. Unfortunately all had been burned, except, of course, Mme Gaillac and myself. We returned to the village one year ago, for it took four years for the courts to rule in our favor. For four years Mme Gaillac and I traveled from village to village. At first we worked the fields, but soon I began to earn money as a midwife and healer. Raymond traveled for months, describing us, asking after us, until he found us and brought us back a year ago.

Our land was returned to my family and it is now my brothers' and mine and Raymond's. Raymond and I were married as soon as I returned to the village. I have taken

Mama's place in the village as midwife and healer. But some-times I worry that I could suffer the same fate as her. Already I am seen by the villagers as different: a survivor where others perished; a healer, a midwife, a woman treated with respect by her husband. Does that put me in the same danger Mama was in? Could this happen all over again? I don't know how to change into a safer person, so I simply carry on.

As for my uncles, we all still live in the same village, but we do not speak. I am civil to Marguerite and have tried to forgive my neighbors, but God has placed a heavy burden on me in that regard. I try to forgive, every day I try. Only Raymond knows of my part in Mama's death. I wanted to share it with my brothers, but I knew that if they heard the whole story, their rage would make them vengeful. They might have killed Uncle Fabrisse or Father Bernard, and then I would lose them to the hangman. I was not about to lose any more loved ones, so it is a secret Raymond and I carry. Father Bernard, at any rate, does not live in this village any-more. After the ruling he was forced to leave by the husbands and sons of the murdered women.

Other villages and towns were not as lucky as ours. Most of the women burned have not had their names cleared, and I have heard that in some villages, by the time the witch-hunter had finished his work, there were no more women or girls left alive.

Perhaps some good person will find this document one day and remember what was done, and remember the poor women like my mama, whose only crime seemed to be that they were born female.

Signed this day in the year 1605 by Mme Rose Gaillac.

Carol Matas is an internationally acclaimed author of over thirty-five novels for children and young adults. Her best-selling work, which includes three award-winning series, has been translated into many languages.

Carol has won many awards including the Geoffrey Bilson Award, the inaugural Silver Birch Award and the Jewish Book Award. Her books have appeared on numerous honor lists, such as the ALA notable list, the *New York Times* notable list and the New York Public Library list for the Teen Age. She has also been nominated twice for a Governor General's Award. Carol lives in Winnipeg, Manitoba, with her husband.

More information about Carol is available on her website: www.carolmatas.com